BLACK SUN

A BREED THRILLER

CAMERON CURTIS

INKUBATOR
BOOKS

Published by Inkubator Books
www.inkubatorbooks.com

ISBN (eBook): 978-1-83756-274-9
ISBN (Paperback): 978-1-83756-275-6

With some inspiration from
Ernest Hemingway

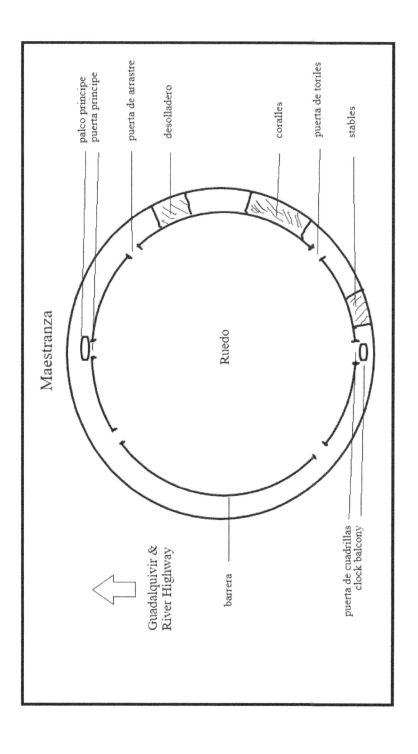

Maestranza

Guadalquivir & River Highway

palco principe
puerta principe
puerta de arrastre
desolladero
corailes
puerta de toriles
stables

Ruedo

barrera

puerta de cuadrillas
clock balcony

1

RODILHAN – PALM SUNDAY, AFTERNOON

Rodilhan is one of the few places in France where one can watch a genuine Spanish bullfight. Bullfighting has been banned in most of France, but here, in the south, the tradition carries on. This picturesque little village lies in the Camargue, within easy driving distance of Arles. I sit at an outdoor café, enjoying a beer. It's Palm Sunday, the first day of Holy Week.

My phone buzzes, and I check my messages. It's Anya Stein. In her early thirties, she's the youngest Deputy Director in the Central Intelligence Agency. Daughter of a Wall Street private equity king. Her grandfather is a wealthy Lithuanian Jew who escaped the Soviet Union. He gave the Stein Center to Harvard. She's attractive, ambitious, and... I have to say it... a bit nerdy.

I suppose one could say we're friends, except she occasionally brings me contract work. The kind of work suitable for an ex-Special Forces operator.

Is now a good time?

I tap on the keyboard. *Sure, call me.*

The phone buzzes and I lift it to my ear. "How are you enjoying your bonus?" Stein asks.

"It's great, Stein. The hotel is first class. You didn't have to do that."

"After that last job, you deserve it. What are you up to?"

"Having a drink in a nice outdoor café. In about an hour, I'll be going to a bullfight."

"You mean where they kill the poor defenseless bull?"

"That poor defenseless bull has two sharp horns he uses like a boxer."

"A boxer?"

"Yes. These bulls literally fake you out with their left and stab you with their right. Or the other way around. They weigh somewhere between one and two tons, charge at forty miles an hour, and can throw a matador thirty feet across the ring."

"Well, it's your vacation. Try to enjoy some good wine while you're over there. Send pictures. Sailboats, beaches, cocktails. No bullfighting please... unless they're pics of cute matadors in skintight outfits."

"Those are called *trajes de luces*—suits of lights. What are *you* up to?"

"The Russians are mopping the floor with our guys, and the head shed doesn't know what to do. Enemy artillery is killing a thousand men a day."

By *our guys*, Stein means the Ukrainian army. They are overmatched, fighting to repel Russian attacks. The Ukrainian conflict is a conventional war. As Deputy Director of Special Situations, there isn't much scope for Stein to make a difference.

"Stein, you're part of the head shed."

"Sometimes, I forget. I'd rather be out there with the guys."

Stein's heart will always be with field operators. I've seen her in action.

"Get them to make peace. This war has gone on way too long."

"That's a conversation we can have when you get back. Enjoy your vacation."

Stein disconnects the call.

Vacations are meant to be escapes. I'll watch a bullfight this afternoon, then make my way to Spain. Play things by ear, arrive in Seville in time for Easter Sunday. The Holy Week— Semana Santa—is a tradition in Spain. Seville is the spiritual capital of bullfighting. The city's bullring, the *Maestranza*, is the oldest and most beautiful in Spain, if not the world. By tradition, Easter Sunday, the day of Resurrection, marks the opening of the Seville bullfighting season. I plan to be there.

I turn my phone to landscape mode, prop it on the graceful metalwork table, and stream the news.

The war in Ukraine continues to hold the world's attention. The Russians call it a Special Military Operation, but let's call a spade a spade. Bullets, artillery shells, and missiles are flying. People are getting killed. It's a war. The Ukrainians are getting the worst of it, and they are begging NATO for money and weapons.

I know former Special Forces operators who volunteered to fight on the Ukrainian side. They invited me to join them, but I politely declined. Between executive protection jobs and Stein's contracts, I see enough action to make a living. I'm sympathetic to the Ukrainian cause. It isn't that I don't *want* to fight. One man can't make a difference in the kind of industrial-scale war the Russians and Ukrainians are waging.

No, I need a vacation. Time to travel at my own pace and see places I want to see. Let others fight this war.

Coverage switches to the recent coup d'etat in Marethia, a small principality in the Carpathians. The little country lies between Hungary and Ukraine. In fact, it was once part of the Austro-Hungarian Empire and retained a government ruled by the prince, with administrative powers delegated to a small parliament.

For decades, Marethia remained peaceful. The prince kept the country scrupulously neutral. He resisted pressure from the prime minister to join the European Union. Marethia earned income from its position as a tax haven. Subordinating its interests to the financial regulations of any large bloc would destroy its financial industry.

The Palvet Pass connects Marethia to Ukraine. The pass is the only route through the Carpathians that can be used year-round to transport weapons from Romania to Ukraine. The prince had been under pressure from NATO to allow the transfer of weapons through the pass. He remained firm in his neutrality.

It's been well over a week since the prince and the royal family were massacred. They were herded into the courtyard of their home and shot. New videos of the murder scene have emerged. Cable news shows them, with bodies and blood blurred out. The regent, who should rule in the absence of the royal family, has fled to Hungary. The prime minister is struggling to establish a new government.

The blur does little to hide the graphic nature of the scene. The imagery has been presented to titillate. The commentary paints the prince as an archaic personality, inflexible and obstructive. The report paints the Marethian people as thirsting for democracy, and the prime minister is prepared to provide it.

I close the news stream and set the phone face down on the table. Marethia's story is an old one. History doesn't repeat, but it rhymes. I'm here to get away from wars and rumors of wars. People are walking past me, following the narrow, paved street to the bullring. I drain my beer and join the crowd.

THE BULLRING in Rodilhan looks nothing like the stone Roman amphitheaters in Arles and Nimes. Nothing like the great bullrings of Madrid and Seville. Rodilhan looks like an outdoor venue one might find in Kansas. A circular field, the *ruedo*, extends sixty yards across. The *ruedo* is surrounded by a painted wooden fence, the *barrera*. There is a narrow passage between the *barrera* and the bleachers. Matadors and their assistants, called *peóns*, seek protection behind the fence when faced with difficult situations. Gates in the *barrera* allow men and animals to pass in and out.

It's the bleachers that make Rodilhan a Class 3 bullring. They seat fewer than five thousand and are built from long wooden planks set in metal frames. That doesn't make the fans any less passionate.

My seat is in the front row, overlooking the *barrera*, midway between the main gate and the officials' box. I sit on the hard plank and settle in to watch the event. It's going to be a Spanish bullfight, a *corrida*, where the bull is killed. In France, this is called the *mise-a-morte*. It's more controversial than the *course camarguese*, in which a white ribbon is fastened between the bull's horns. A group of men dodge around the bewildered animal, trying to snatch the ribbon.

The *corrida* is about to start. Two constables, the *aguacillilos*, mounted on fine white horses, approach the president's box. The senior man doffs his cap to the president and pretends to catch an imaginary key. It symbolizes the key to the *corrales*, where the bulls are kept. The president has given his permission to start. The two men walk their horses backwards to the formation of bullfighters.

There is a crash of cymbals, and the band plays a rousing, passionate tune. The music is amplified by speakers mounted on tall posts that surround the ring. The procession of matadors marches onto the *ruedo* through a gate on my left. There are three matadors and their teams. Each matador leads two *peóns*, two picadors on horseback, and three *banderilleros*.

Javier Rincón, the world's greatest matador, leads the parade. Resplendent in his suit of lights, he stands six feet tall, lean and muscular. His shoulders are thrown back, and his chin is tilted at the perfect angle to convey confidence without appearing arrogant. The archetypical matador was a starving child, with the drive and talent to reach the heights of wealth and fame. Fifty years old, Rincón looks like he was born an aristocrat.

I came to watch him perform.

At my hotel in Arles, the concierge told me only *course camarguese* were performed in the city. To watch a *mise-a-morte* I would have to go to Rodilhan. However, as luck would have it, the greatest matador alive, Javier Rincón, would perform on Palm Sunday. In Spain and Mexico, aficionados argued his position among the greats. Compared him to Manolete, Arruza and Belmonte. No, some said, Rincón is great, but *those* are the immortals.

Three matadors, six bulls. The most senior matador fights the first and fourth bulls. A gate opens, and Rincón's first bull charges into the ring and stops. The animal is black, mid-sized, about a ton in weight. He turns to examine the gate through which he entered, then looks around the ring.

Rincón's *peóns* cape the bull. They attract its attention by waving the cloth before its eyes. Bulls are nearsighted. Their attention is drawn to color and movement. That is how bull-fighters deceive and dominate them.

Some bulls are harder to dominate than others. *Toros bravos*—brave bulls—are prized for their aggression. They give a good fight. Matadors draw their bulls by random chance. The best matador can go an entire season without finding a bull that allows him to showcase his talent.

This is a good bull, but not great. The *peóns* cape the animal into position for the picadors. The men carry lances and ride horses protected by padded body armor. Armor was introduced in 1928. Prior to that, horses were frequently gored. The picadors lance the bull, driving the pics into the great hump of muscle behind the animal's neck. The purpose is to weaken it to even the odds for the matador.

The picadors do a good job. The bull charges the horses, rams their body armor, and pushes them into the *barrera*. While the bull is straining against the horse, the lancer stabs it with the pic.

My eyes search the *barrera* for Rincón. I see him standing with his arms folded over the fence. With critical eyes, he watches the *peóns* and picadors work the bull. He straightens, goes to one of his *banderilleros* and takes the *banderillas,* a pair of wooden darts, from the man. The stakes are two feet long, with barbed points, and adorned with colored ribbons.

The crowd stirs. Normally the *banderilleros* perform the second act of the bullfight. This is the Third of Flags where the colorful stakes are driven into the shoulders of the bull. Sometimes, to display his prowess, the matador performs this act himself.

Rincón marches onto the *ruedo*. "*¡Hoy! ¡Toro!*"

The bull needs little urging. The man is making an easy target of himself. Rincón approaches straight on, a dart in each hand, held at one end of the stake. He raises them over his head, prepares to plunge them *over* the bull's horns.

Foaming at the mouth, the bull snorts and paws the earth. Like a sprinter coming out of the blocks, the animal charges. Its acceleration is explosive.

Rincón stops, stands with his feet together, and rises on his toes. Greets the bull with the *banderillas* raised. When it seems the man has waited too long, and the bull must crash into him, Rincón springs aside. The bull's great head and horns miss him by inches, and the matador drives the darts into the beast's flesh.

"*¡Olé!*" the crowd roars.

Enraged, the animal screeches to a stop and wheels on Rincón. The matador is already gone, back to the *barrera*, where he collects the second pair of *banderillas*.

The bull stands no more than twenty feet from me. I can see blood pumping from the pic wounds in its torn hide. The animal has been weakened, but the *banderillas* are doing their job. The darts are enraging the bull for the final act of the *corrida*, the Third of Death. It is in that act that the bull-fighter kills the bull with a curved sword, the *estoque*.

Rincón approaches the bull a second time, holding the banderillas with a light touch. This time, the bull is crafty. Animals learn, and a good bull studies his opponent just as the matador studies the bull. The animal circles around to Rincón's left. The maneuver places the matador between the bull and the *barrera*.

I don't like the looks of this. No more than ten feet away, Rincón has presented his back to me. He's boxed in.

The bull snorts and charges. Rincón rises on his toes. At the last instant, he springs to the left and drives the darts home. The bull bellows. Rincón lands on his feet, but his slipper slides on the loose earth and he crashes heavily to the ground.

A collective gasp issues from the crowd. The bull slams into the *barrera* with a terrific crash. Wheels around, looking for its tormentor.

Rincón is on the ground, scrambling to his feet. The *peóns*, who must rush in to distract the bull, are too far away.

Leaping onto the guard rail, I hurdle the width of the passageway and plant my right foot on the top of the *barrera*. My momentum carries me forward, and I land on the *ruedo* between Rincón and the bull.

Driven by instinct and reflex, I have no idea what to do. The bull's great head is swinging toward me, the long horns flashing. I strike the animal on its snout with the heel of my right hand.

With a bellow, the animal recoils, then wheels toward me. I run like hell. If I dash back to my seat, the bull will have time to turn on Rincón. Instead, I make for a spot on the *barrera* thirty feet away. I look back, find the bull gaining. My ears are filled with a tidal wave of sound, a roar that swells from a thousand throats.

I hit the *barrera*, put my hands on the top, and vault the barrier as the bull crashes into the fence.

Rincón's *peóns* arrive at the scene and cape the bull away. The matador straightens with grave dignity. His eyes sweep the crowd. Then he doffs his black *montera* hat and extends it to me. As one, the spectators rise to their feet and cheer.

Men in the passageway clap me on my back and shoulders. Guide me to my seat, help me climb onto the bleachers. When I look for Rincón, I see he has returned to the gate. He exchanges words with an older man, who first hands him a red cape, the *muleta*. Then, into Rincón's hands, the man places the *estoque*.

It is time for the last act, the Third of Death.

2

RODILHAN – PALM SUNDAY, EVENING

Rincón has killed two bulls. They were not very good bulls, but neither were they very bad. The first bull was the better of the two. I don't say that only because it offered me my brief moment of glory. The bull was genuinely brave, and the encouragement of Rincón's *banderillas* brought out the best in him.

I'll go further. The bull I punched was the best of the *corrida*. This isn't boasting. The statistics bear it out. Aficionados generally concur—of any six bulls in a *corrida*, only one satisfies. Only one allows the matador an opportunity to display his art. There are three bullfighters in the typical *corrida*, each fighting two bulls. Therefore, the chances of a given matador drawing the best bull are poor.

The odds go up if the bulls are from a great ranch, such as that of Miura. That is why the name of the bull ranch is prominently displayed on the poster that advertises the *corrida*. The bulls are stars, as much as the matadors.

Mano-a-mano describes a *corrida* in which two matadors

fight three bulls each. In such a case, the matador has a higher chance of drawing the best bull.

Aficionados agree that only twenty percent of *corridas* are worth attending. Five percent are memorable. One percent are great. And yet, the drawing of the bulls and matadors is random. Their passion for the *corrida* is so intense, the aficionados continue to pay their money. Each ticket is a gamble that they will be fortunate enough to witness the one in a hundred performance they can tell their grandchildren about.

Rincón dispatched the fourth bull with as much panache as the poor animal allowed. Doffed his *montera* and marched from the ring like a prince.

The last fight of the day starts. The day has already been a memorable experience for my vacation. I wonder if I should stay to watch the matador kill the bull.

"Excuse me, señor."

I look at the man in a bullfighter costume, who has approached me from the passageway behind the *barrera*. "Yes?"

"I am Allegre," the man says. "Picador for Maestro Rincón."

"I'm Breed," I tell him. Reach down to shake his hand.

"The maestro sends his thanks for your intervention earlier. He would be honored if you would join him for drinks and a meal this evening."

"It is *my* honor. Please tell the maestro that I accept."

Allegre hands me a card. It is in French, but someone has written a translation in English and Spanish on the back. "The maestro will be here at nine o'clock this evening."

The picador nods gravely to me and hurries away.

· · ·

I DECIDE to watch the last fight. Each bullfight lasts twenty minutes, so a full *corrida* typically takes two hours. Can't believe my good fortune. Had I left early, I would have missed Rincón's invitation.

The departure of the crowd is a casual affair. It's not a mob scene, like eighty thousand spectators leaving a US football stadium. The people who come to Rodilhan for the *mise-le-mort* are an amiable bunch.

Many came from Arles and Nimes. The remainder are locals, and I follow them down the narrow, picturesque street. I find myself walking with a family of four. A middle-aged couple, their son, and his wife. I examine the address on the card and show it to the older gentleman. *Le Petit Lapin*, the card says.

The man laughs. "We are going there," he says. "Come with us."

Looks like the whole town is going to *Le Petit Lapin*. It's not far. A two-story wooden building on the main street. There's a wide front, with a porch and three steps leading from the front parking lot. There are spaces for about fifteen cars, with access on either side. Behind the building is a larger lot with more parking.

A red neon sign advertises *Le Petit Lapin, Bar Café*.

Inside, a white-haired man with a handlebar mustache is playing an accordion. A younger man sits next to him, on a straight-backed chair, playing a banjo. The locals dance and drink wine.

My eye is drawn to a low mezzanine to one side of the room. Rincón sits at the head of a table, drinking with five men. Allegre is there. He has been keeping an eye out for me. The picador waves and gets up to escort me to the table.

"Maestro, may I present Mr Breed." Allegre lightly touches

my arm. "Mr Breed, this is our maestro, Javier Rincón, the greatest matador in Spain. And *that* means—the world."

Rincón rises to his feet and appraises me. Shakes my hand. "Mr Breed. *El espontáneo.* You stole the show."

"Hardly, Maestro. There was no time to think."

"Sometimes that is the way, is it not. But you understand. The *corrida* is first and foremost a spectacle. You gave us all something special today. More than those silly cows could provide."

There is a lot of wine on the table, and many appetizers. Allegre pours wine for me, and I drink deeply. "A lot depends on the bull, doesn't it?"

"Breed, once a matador reaches a certain level in his art —*everyth*ing depends on the bull."

"That's what we say," I tell him. "It is better to be lucky than good."

"*Sí.*" One of the *banderilleros* raises his glass in a toast. "*Suerte.* Luck is everything."

"I took your moment today, my friend." Rincón claps the *banderillero* on the shoulder. Typically the picadors and *banderilleros* prepare the bull for the matador. The *banderillero* enjoys an opportunity to put on a show. Some matadors like to show off their own skill. Rincón is one such. The *banderillero* is not willing to begrudge his boss's prerogative.

"It was a pleasure to watch you plant the darts, Maestro."

Of course it was. I watched old films of Carlos Arruza working with the *banderillas*. His agility and grace were otherworldly. Rincón is good, but his work with the *banderillas* is not in Arruza's class.

We speak about bullfighting for hours. At last, the picadors and the *banderilleros* get up to leave. They explain that they have to prepare for their trip to Valencia the next morning. Allegre is the last to go. He addresses Rincón carefully. "Shall I stay, Maestro? Do you need help?"

Hard to believe Allegre is the designated driver. We've all been drinking. The tabletop is strewn with empty wine bottles.

Rincón shakes his head. "No, my friend. You get some rest. There is much to do in the morning."

I watch Allegre hurry to join his friends. I reach for a bottle and drink more wine. Sit with Maestro Rincón and speak of bulls.

"What you did today is the dream of many poor young boys in Spain," he says.

"In what way?"

"Boys dream of becoming matadors. They play as matadors and bulls from their youngest years. If they have skill— and sadly, even if they do not—they dream of an opportunity to enter the ring. They dream of being noticed by a promoter, who will launch their careers."

"If they are not killed."

Rincón smiles broadly. "*Or* arrested. Such an act is against the law."

The matador tops up my wine glass. "Now tell me, Breed. Where do *you* find courage?"

I sip the wine to give myself time to consider the question. "I don't think about it. I do the work that needs to be done, let the chips fall where they may."

"Spoken like a soldier," Rincón says. "Once on the *ruedo*, the field of battle, one does what must be done. And before the battle?"

"Everybody's afraid. It's part of the job."

"Bravo." Rincón raises his glass to me. "We are not so different, you and I."

"Perhaps not." I'm uncomfortable talking about things like fear and courage. They have always seemed things to be experienced, not spoken about. "Maestro, thank you for a wonderful evening. I must go."

"Why?"

"I want to find a place to spend the night in Rodilhan," I say. "I will return to Arles tomorrow."

Rincón leans back in his chair and draws a Havana cigar from his jacket pocket. Takes out a gold cigar cutter and prepares to smoke. "As you wish, Breed. I will enjoy a bit more wine and music."

I get up and shake his hand. "Thank you, Maestro. You've made my visit a memorable one."

"Come to Seville next week," Rincón smiles. "At the *Maestranza*, I shall kill two Miura bulls. I will give you a show."

3

RODILHAN – PALM SUNDAY, EVENING

The evening air is cool and fresh. I step onto the front porch of the bar, listen to the strains of festive music coming from inside. Through the blinds, I catch glimpses of men and women dancing past the windows. I need to find an inn for the night. I lean against a post at the front steps. Enjoy the feeling of having the freedom to do what I want.

A blue Mercedes SUV is parked to one side of the bar's front lot. It's shiny in the glow of streetlights. I notice it because it's occupying two parking spaces in a small lot that's already full. There are five people in the vehicle. Two men in front. Two more in the back, with a girl sitting between them.

The man in the right rear passenger seat stares out the window at me. Dark and brooding, he has black, shoulder-length hair and a droopy mustache. It's the man's eyes that get my attention. They're merciless eyes. The kind of eyes you see in hardened career criminals. Men who are capable of anything.

I'm relaxed, soaking up the romance of southern France. The man with the mustache makes me imagine a Gypsy King. I look away from him, because I don't want trouble. When I look back, he's turned his attention to the other occupants of the SUV. Yes, I say to myself, he's some kind of Gypsy King, and those men belong to his band.

The trouble is, I can't ignore the instincts I've developed over years of training and combat. The men in front have the same hard look. Both are swarthy. The driver's wearing a brown leather jacket. The man in the right front passenger seat wears his hair in a man-bun. The driver looks bored. The man-bun scowls like he's pissed off at the world. I can't see the face of the man sitting behind the driver. He's sitting too far back. I can tell he's a man only by his bulk. He and the Gypsy King have the girl crushed between them.

Pale and blond, the girl stands out as an incongruity among the hard men. From her head and shoulders, I can tell she's a tiny thing in her mid-teens. Her gaze is vacant. She's detached from her surroundings, apart from the men who surround her.

Everything about the group in the SUV spells trouble.

Four men approach from the direction of the general store next to the bar. With a determined stride, they cross the narrow side street that separates the buildings. They walk directly to the front of the SUV. My eyes register them with a glance.

This group is led by a big man with a barrel chest and a shovel beard. He's six feet tall, in his fifties, with salt-and-pepper hair. He's wearing a black leather car coat that extends past his hips. The other three men are younger. Thirties or forties. Leather jackets, car coats.

The men in the car start to move. The driver starts the

engine, the others reach for weapons. The movement of their shoulders telegraphs their intentions. They're too late, because the four men in front of the vehicle are the first to draw. They produce weapons from under their jackets.

The big guy with the beard produces a Beretta 92. Two of the younger men whip out Spanish Z84 submachine guns. "Corto," or short models, they're designed for commando use. Twenty-five round magazines, 9mm Parabellum. Stripped of their folding stocks, the weapons are easily concealed under car coats.

Before the men in the car can react, the attackers open fire. The submachine guns chatter, fired from the hip. Bullets rake the front windshield of the SUV. The gypsies in front jerk like puppets on strings. The man-bun in the front passenger seat struggles against the hail of lead and pushes his door open. Bloody holes are ripped in his cheeks, nose, the side of his head. Pistol in hand, he spills sideways and hangs halfway out of the car.

There's no cover on the porch. I run to the row of parked cars and duck behind the engine compartment of a Citroën sedan.

The rear doors of the SUV swing open. The man in the left passenger seat gets out, raises an H&K MP5. He cuts down the two attackers on the left—a man with a pistol, and one of the two men firing Z84s.

The bearded man and the other submachine gunner turn their weapons on the new threat. The left passenger window of the SUV shatters and bullets stitch the car door. The man cries out and falls backward onto the pavement.

Cars don't provide cover against gunfire. The only bullet-proof parts of a car are the engine block, door posts, axels, and wheel rims. Unless the vehicle's been up-armored, the windows, side panels and doors provide no protection.

Swearing, the Gypsy King lunges from the vehicle. He's got a small pistol in his right hand. It looks like a toy in his paw. A Beretta Cheetah. Low capacity, .380 ACP, slow rate of fire. That's a tiny bullet in a low-powered cartridge. The Gypsy King relies on henchmen to carry the heavy artillery.

I bet he wishes he had more than a Saturday Night Special. He ducks behind the open car door and fires one-handed. The tiny round hits the submachine gunner in the throat and blood squirts from the hole. No stopping power. The submachine gunner turns his weapon on the Gypsy King even as crimson jets splash his weapon.

The gypsy with the MP5 isn't dead. He struggles to one knee, dumps his mag on the bleeding submachine gunner.

Like a ghost, the thin girl crawls from the SUV. She lands on her hands and knees behind the Gypsy King. Finds her feet, runs along the row of parked cars. Shit, she's heading right for me.

The big guy with the shovel beard realizes he's all alone. He raises his Beretta 92. The gypsy with the MP5 is out of ammo. The weapon has such a high rate of fire it empties in a second. The bearded man shoots him in the face.

With a grunt, the Gypsy King half-turns, sees the girl running away. The man with the shovel beard deliberately aims his weapon at the running girl's back. The Gypsy King fires the Cheetah again. The man with the beard jerks as the bullet strikes him in the left shoulder. Spoils his aim.

I grab the girl by the arm as she runs past me. Drag her behind the engine compartment of the Citroën. The man with the shovel beard goes on firing. He pumps three rounds in our direction, another two at the Gypsy King.

A police siren wails in the distance. Rodilhan is a small village. They rely on the gendarmerie. I have no idea what their response time will be.

Neither do the gunmen. The man with the shovel beard runs to the general store.

Conflicted, the Gypsy King looks back along the row of parked cars. Our eyes meet over their hoods. He decides to cut his losses. Crawls around to the front passenger seat and hauls the dead body of man-bun out of the SUV. Crawls inside.

With a low thrum, the SUV lurches forward. The Gypsy King must be lying across the front seat. He's thrown the vehicle into drive. With his left hand, he pushes the dead driver back in his seat and manipulates the steering wheel. With his right, he presses the accelerator.

Slowly, the Gypsy King drives the vehicle onto the side street. The bearded man empties his magazine into the front grille and what's left of the windshield. Drops the empty mag and reloads.

When he reaches the main drag, the Gypsy King leans on the gas. Pokes his head up and tries to keep the SUV moving in a straight line.

An engine growls and a big car lurches to a stop behind me. It's a huge, gray Mercedes 450 SEL sedan. The kind built in the '70s with real leather seats, it's an expensive luxury classic. Rincón is at the wheel. He leans over and opens the passenger door.

"Breed, get in."

The bearded man turns on us, raises the Beretta 92. He fires, and bullets skid off the hoods of the parked cars.

Like a tiny bird, the girl quivers. I grab her by the arms and pick her up. She feels weightless. I shove her into the car, pile in after her, and slam the door. There's a clang as one of the 9mm bullets drills the Mercedes.

Rincón accelerates out of the parking lot. Drives in the direction of Arles.

I twist in my seat and look back. The Gypsy King and the SUV are gone. The big man with the shovel beard is nowhere to be seen. All that's left of the engagement are dead bodies and weapons strewn over the parking lot.

Across the street from the bar, a man steps from the shadows. He stares at us as we drive away. Looks like he's memorizing Rincón's license plate.

The man's face is lit in the glow of the streetlamps. It's a familiar face, but I can't place him.

Rincón turns a corner and we leave the scene behind.

4

ARLES – PALM SUNDAY, LATE EVENING

Rincón eases up on the accelerator. We don't want to attract attention on the road to Arles. Police cars zoom toward us. They flash past, and the wail of their sirens fades with the Doppler effect. "Was the girl shot?" he asks.

I inspect the girl for wounds.

She hasn't been shot. She's wearing a plain white T-shirt, blue jeans, and white tennis shoes. No bullet holes in her clothing, no blood. But her eyes are glazed, and she's shivering.

There are needle marks in the crooks of her elbows and on her forearms. I examine them—a pair of marks on her left arm are fresh. The remainder are fading. Most important, no scars. The tracks aren't more than two weeks old.

"I don't think so," I tell Rincón. "She's on something. Heroin, I think."

To the girl I say, "Are you alright? What's wrong?"

Unresponsive, the girl stares at me through pinpoint

pupils. It's dark—they should be dilated. They're pinned by the drug.

"We have to take her to the police," Rincón says.

The girl jerks. "No police. Please."

The girl's reaction is so violent I put my arm around her. She cringes, then settles against me. "Why not?" I ask.

"No police," she says. "No police."

"What is your name?"

The girl struggles to engage her mind. "Julia," she says.

Something's wrong. Not because eight men with submachine guns shot each other in front of us. The bearded man tried to shoot this girl in the back. More disturbing, the image of the man standing in the street nags my memory. I know I've seen him before.

"Can you drive me to my hotel?" I ask Rincón.

"No police?"

"No police." I need time to figure things out.

"You need help," Rincón says. "I will take you to mine."

"Your car is distinctive," I say. "Is it well known in Rodilhan?"

"Yes, I suppose so."

"The last two men saw us leave. This car has one of their bullets in it."

"An annoyance, Breed."

"My point is that it will not be difficult for them to learn who the girl left with. It is possible they will find you."

Rincón frowns. "Alright. Where are you staying?"

I give him the name of my hotel and the address.

The bullfighter chuckles. "We are staying at the same hotel, Breed. The most expensive in Arles."

Perks of a Stein bonus. She books me into *her* kind of hotels. I'd be happy at a Holiday Inn.

"I appreciate your help," I say. "We must keep her in *my* room. And *you* must understand that you could be in danger."

The matador takes out his mobile phone and punches a speed dial. Speaks rapidly in Spanish.

"Who were those men?" I ask the girl.

The girl lifts her face to me. It's a thin face, with big eyes, high cheekbones, and a wide mouth. She's pretty, but her features are drawn. There are dark circles around her eyes. She looks like she's wearing a mask. "Leandro," she says.

We left six dead bodies in that parking lot. "Who's Leandro?"

Julia looks up at me. Again, her mind appears to work in slow motion. She raises her hand to her face. Makes a motion with her thumb and forefinger. Like she's stroking a mustache.

"The man with a mustache?"

Julia nods. Returns her head to my chest, closes her eyes.

Rincón pockets his phone. "I have advised my manager to prepare for our arrival. Obviously, we cannot carry the girl through the lobby in this condition. He will meet us at the service entrance. Who is this Leandro?"

"He's the leader of the men in the car. Long hair, mustache, looks like a gypsy. He got away."

"And the others?"

"I don't know. Maybe the girl can tell us more."

"When she wakes?" Julia is fast asleep, her face against my chest.

"I don't know." Rincón's attention is focused on the road. I study his aristocratic profile. A handsome man, a sculptor could make a fine bust of him. Or a statue of a matador dressed in a suit of lights. "I think she'll have to kick her addiction first."

"Are you sure she's addicted?"

"Her sluggishness is a sign that she's had an injection recently. She'll go into withdrawal within six hours. Then we can judge the extent of her addiction."

"You have seen this?"

"Yes. The easiest things to get in Afghanistan are heroin and bullets."

Rincón accepts this and we fall into silence. Julia sleeps, but every few minutes she quivers or shakes. Troubled, I close my eyes and struggle to reconstruct the image of the man in the street.

As far as I can tell, there are three parties interested in Julia. The Gypsy King, the bearded man, and the lone figure in the street. Three different parties with unclear motives.

This was supposed to be a vacation.

ARLES IS A BEAUTIFUL CITY. The streets around the amphitheater are picturesque, the architecture medieval. There are few buildings taller than three or four stories. Our hotel is easy to find. Clean and modern, it stands six stories high. Its top floor suites enjoy a panoramic view of the city.

Rincón drives around the hotel and approaches from the service entrance. It's late, and the loading bay is deserted. There's a large garage, and room for vans and trucks to back up against a raised concrete platform.

A door on the platform opens and two men step out to meet us. One is old and gaunt. He wears a dark brown wool sweater with stylish leather patches on the shoulders and elbows. The other man is younger, dressed in jeans and a rough work shirt.

The matador parks the Mercedes and we climb out. Julia stirs against me, but doesn't waken. I pick her up in an arms carry, and we go to the men.

Rincón introduces us. "This is my manager, Salazar. This boy is Curro."

My arms are full, and I nod my greeting. "I'm on the top floor," I tell them.

"So am I," Rincón says. He hands his car keys to Curro. "Park the car. Then return here and watch the loading bay. If anyone suspicious arrives and enters the hotel, call myself or Salazar."

Salazar leads us into the hotel.

"I want a *peón* in the lobby as well," Rincón tells Salazar.

"I have seen to it, Maestro. Alvaro volunteered to stand watch."

We pass the fire stairs and Salazar takes us to a service elevator. We get in and he punches the button for the sixth floor.

The elevator door sucks open and reveals a wide, brightly lit corridor. The service elevator is at the very end, adjacent to a walk-in linen closet and the fire stairs. We step out and Rincón gestures to the right. "I have the corner suite."

"Mine is in the middle."

Both of our rooms overlook the amphitheater, but my room is smaller. It's halfway along the corridor, across from the guest elevator.

I try to wake Julia up. The heroin has pushed her into a deep stupor. Rincón takes her in his arms while I unlock my door. "Put her on the bed," I say.

We step inside, close the door behind us.

"I suggest you and Mr Salazar spend the night in my room. It might not be as grand as your own, but it will be safer. We'll have a better idea of what to do in the morning."

Rincón looks amused. "Where will *you* stay, Breed?"

"I shall spend the night in *your* suite."

"I thought as much. You really expect an attack tonight?"

"Hope for the best, plan for the worst. Without weapons, this floor is indefensible."

"Very well." Rincón hands me his key card. "I have contacts in the Seville police force. I will make one or two discreet calls. Find out if there are any missing girls matching Julia's description."

I take the card and we swap phone numbers.

"Don't let anyone in," I tell him. "Don't step to the door unless the person on the other side calls you first."

5

ARLES - PALM SUNDAY, LATE EVENING

I step into the corridor and walk to Rincón's door. The air smells of air conditioning and freshly steam-cleaned carpet. I swipe the key card and let myself in. My room's nice, but Rincón's is palatial. It's a corner suite, with picture windows along both walls of the sitting room. One window overlooks the Rhône, the other overlooks the amphitheater. Against the night lights of Arles, the Roman structure shines brightly.

I cast my eye around the room. There's a long, cushy sofa with matching side chairs. The coffee and side tables are modern, with clear glass set in shiny metal frames. There's a dining table to the right, set for four. It's next to one of the picture windows. The guests can dine and enjoy the view.

The dining table is separated from the kitchen by a low counter. The kitchen looks well equipped. I'll look at it later.

I cast my gaze to the left. A door leads into the bedroom. I push the door open and go inside. King-size bed, wall-mounted TV, ensuite bathroom with a hot tub. There's a large closet, a fold-out ironing board and a flatiron. I take the flatiron and disconnect the electrical cord from the appliance. Wind it into a coil and stuff it in my hip pocket.

I leave the light on in the bedroom. Go back into the sitting room, close the door. Rummage around the kitchen. There's a fridge and a proper oven. The suite has been built for guests who want a home away from home for a month.

The fridge is well stocked with bottles of wine and ice water. I pour myself a glass of water and drink it in one gulp. Pour myself another.

There's a carving board and a block of knives. I draw the carving knife and examine it. Solingen steel, eight inches long, with a full tang. The thin blade suits me fine. I wish it had a guard, but you can't always get what you want.

A set of frying pans hangs from hooks on the wall. Looks like they've never been used. I pick up the biggest one. It's eight inches across, weighs three or four pounds.

I swallow another drink of water, take the frying pan and carving knife back into the sitting room.

SOCP—Special Operations Combatives Program—is a course in close quarters combat for assaulters. They teach you to use ordinary, everyday contents of a house to channel adversaries down "fatal funnels." When men enter a room, they tend to step around furniture. They don't think twice. Like a minefield, you can use furniture to create area control obstacles.

As assaulters, when we enter a room, we're trained to *ignore* obstacles presented by furniture. If a sofa is in your way, go over it instead of around. The point is, you're trained to see a room differently. We move from Point A to Point B the way *we* want to, not the way the enemy wants us to.

I drag the sofa closer to the front door so it obstructs the most direct path to the big picture windows. Rearrange the side tables and chairs. One side chair obstructs the path to the kitchen. I place the other so it leaves the way clear to the bedroom.

I stand at the front door and close the lights. The sitting room and kitchen are dark. The room is illuminated only by the sky outside and the sparkling lights of Arles. To the left, a narrow beam of light is visible under the bedroom door. Satisfied, I go to the dining room table and pick up one of the straight-backed chairs. Carry it to the front door.

The door opens inward to the right. I set the chair down on that side, back to the wall. Make myself comfortable. Lay the knife and frying pan on the floor next to me, settle in to wait.

MY MOBILE PHONE BUZZES. It's Rincón.

"Alvaro says two men are on their way up," the matador says. "They bribed the desk clerk for my suite number."

"Thanks."

"Do you need help?"

"No, stay with the girl. Whatever happens, don't leave the room."

I pocket the phone, get to my feet, and stand with my back to the wall. I leave enough room for the door to swing open. I carry the carving knife in my left hand, blade up. Hold the frying pan in my right hand, bottom facing away from me. Take a deep breath.

The men are quiet when they come. They push a flat metal strip between the door jamb and the door. Slide a heavy flat-head screwdriver in next to it, force the lock. The door opens and they enter the darkened room. They hold their weapons the way actors do in the movies. Weaver grips with bent elbows. First, one man enters, then the other. They ignore the corners.

The light beneath the bedroom door beckons. They sweep their weapons over the sitting room and kitchen. A cursory sweep. They're more interested in the bedroom. The first man stumbles against the back of the sofa. It's three feet closer to the front door than one would expect. Clumsy, he steps left to the end of the sofa and advances on the bedroom. The number two man follows. They're dark shapes, silhouetted against the picture windows.

Their eyes haven't adapted to the darkness. I take a breath, step forward, and swing the frying pan backhand in a flat arc. Its solid edge smashes into the back of the number two man's neck. There's a whack, and the blow crushes his fourth and fifth cervical vertebrae. It breaks his neck and severs the spine in the space between. The man crumples like a sack of potatoes.

Confused, the first man whirls on me. From my point of view, he's a silhouetted target. All *he* sees before his eyes is a black curtain. In a heartbeat, his face encounters the flat of the pan with a loud clang. The human head weighs eight pounds and I belted one with a four pound steel tennis racket. The vibration from the impact runs straight to my elbow.

The man staggers backward. Without changing my grip, I chop the edge of the pan against the wrist of his gun hand. The long bones—radius and ulna—snap, and he issues a sharp cry. The pistol falls to the floor. The man rocks upright like one of those weighted punching bags that won't stay down.

I swing the weapon again, this time in a horizontal arc. Crack the edge of the pan against the bridge of his nose, right between the eyes. There's a liquid snort as blood explodes from his nostrils. He lands flat on his back, unconscious.

Had I wanted to kill him, I would have struck his throat.

I separate the man from his weapons system. Pick up the guns, turn on the lights.

The pistols look like Colt 1911s, but they're Spanish Modelo BMs. Eight-round magazines, 9mm Parabellum. Respectable weapons with a reasonably high rate of fire, but low capacity. They're accurate at close range. Spanish service pistols, they've also seen combat with the Rhodesian and South African armies. I toss one on the sofa along with the frying pan. Safety the other and squeeze it into my waistband.

I turn and check out the damage.

One man's dead with a broken neck. The other is laid out on his back. His face is a mass of blood from the eyes down. His mouth is open. I stoop and listen to him gurgle. The airway's clear, he'll live. For a while.

I whip out the power cord and bind his wrists. Nice and tight. Drag him by the ankles, plant the straight-backed chair over his chest with the back toward his face. I stroll to the kitchen, swallow another drink of water. Fill the glass and carry it into the sitting room.

Pick up a sofa cushion, stick the carving knife into it. Sit down on the wooden chair with my arms across the top rail. Lay the knife and cushion on the floor next to me. I look down on the unconscious man and slowly pour water on his face. He coughs, sputters, and wakes up. Finds himself immobilized. His legs are free to kick, but with the chair planted on his chest, and me on top, he isn't going anywhere.

"Who are you working for?" I ask.

The man coughs some more. Shakes his head. I draw the knife from the cushion and hold the point to his throat. "I said... who are you working for?"

"*No habla Ingles.*"

"Wrong answer." I stab the knife into the cushion, take out my phone, and open the translator app. "*¿Para quién estás trabajando?*"

The man struggles, tries to shout. I plant the cushion on his face. He drums his heels on the floor. When he lies quiet, I lift the cushion off. Push the point of the knife into his throat, deep enough to draw blood.

"*Digame. ¿Para quién estás trabajando?*"

He's choking. The blood from his smashed nose is running down his trachea. Young guy, late twenties. They start them early in Spain. He coughs, manages to blubber the words, "*El Vasco.*"

"Leandro?"

"*No, no. El Vasco.*"

"Say again. *Otra vez.*"

The boy is weeping. "*El Vasco. Déjame vivir. Amor de dios.*"

That sounds like a good answer. I take out my phone and translate "*El Vasco.*"

The Basque.

I shove the cushion onto the boy's face and press the muzzle of the Model BM against it. Not too firmly, I don't want to push the weapon out of battery. The cushion muffles the shots.

Now the bearded man has a name.

6

I find the linen storage room next to the service elevator. It's unlocked. Thirty minutes later, I've stuffed the two bodies and the bloody cushion down the laundry chute. If they don't get caught in a switchback, they'll spill out somewhere in the basement. If I'm lucky and they *do* get caught in a switchback, they might remain undiscovered for a week.

That would be convenient. Who knows how long it'll be before people ask questions. Why isn't laundry coming down from the sixth floor? Then again, all laundry looks alike. How long will it be before someone notices that laundry arriving at the basement is five-sixths normal?

The power cord goes back on the flatiron. I replace the knife and frying pan in the kitchen. Push the furniture back into place. In the bathroom, I find paper towels and a bottle of bleach under the sink. I clean up the blood on the floor and flush the paper towels down the toilet.

The BM looks like a 1911, but there is an important difference. The BM doesn't have a grip safety. People are comfortable carrying the 1911 cocked and locked with two safeties. Should I trust the BM with only one? If I'm wrong, kids might be a problem. Alright, Condition One it is. I stash the pistol appendix carry, squeeze the other into my hip pocket.

I step into the corridor and freeze. There's a man standing outside my room.

"Well done, Breed." The man is leaning casually against the wall, arms folded. Looks like he's been waiting for me. "I expected nothing less."

The man looks forty, with a blond crew cut. He's wearing khaki pants, a cream shirt, and a dark brown leather jacket. How did he get past Alvaro? Rincón's man was watching the lobby and the elevator. This man took the fire stairs.

Close up, the puzzle pieces click into place. It's been nine years, but Colonel Maxim Orlov hasn't changed. We met at the Battle of Debaltseve, in 2014. I was observing the Ukrainian army, he was advising the separatist militias of Donetsk and Luhansk. The fighting was savage and fluid. It washed back and forth, the entire town was a battlefield.

Ukrainian and Russian units were tangled in savage house-to-house fighting, often hand-to-hand. In the chaos, Orlov and I were separated from our men. Both sides called artillery strikes down on the contested position. By accident, we found a bombed-out basement. Sheltered together, came to an uneasy truce.

Orlov's English was better than my Russian. Over three hours, we got to know each other. Did not find ourselves very different. Ferociously patriotic. Competent specialists in the art of war. When the shelling stopped, we went our separate ways.

"Hello, Orlov." I shift my hand close to the BM.

"That won't be necessary, Breed. I'm here to talk."

The Russian speaks flawless English with a slight German accent. An officer of the 45th Guards Spetznaz. Based in Moscow, detached for special operations.

My hand doesn't move. "Alright," I say. "What do you want?"

"Isn't it obvious? I want the girl."

"Who is she?"

Orlov's expression doesn't change. "If you don't know, her identity is of no consequence to you. I have seen you protect her. All that matters is that I will protect her also."

"She's an addict."

"I thought as much. She will receive the best treatment."

"Why?"

"Not your concern."

This conversation is going nowhere. The Russian Federation only sends Maxim Orlov on missions of the highest national interest. "Sorry, Colonel. Unless I get answers, you'll have to take her."

Orlov shrugs. Slowly unfolds his arms, pushes the elevator button. "Not now."

The doors open, and he steps inside. Without another word, he waits for the doors to close. The down arrow lights, and the colonel is gone. I let my breath out and lower my hand.

I TAKE out my phone and call Rincón. "Breed," he says. "*Digame.*"

"Open the door."

Rincón lets me into my room and we swap key cards. Julia is stretched out on the bed, sleeping. Salazar has taken off her shoes and thrown a blanket over her.

"I have inquired about missing girls," Rincón says.

"Any hits?"

"My contact will call me in the morning. He expects a thousand hits."

"Not a surprise, given high youth unemployment."

"Indeed."

I take the pistols from my waistband. "Do you know how to use these?"

"I am better with a rifle, but... yes."

The pistol I used earlier has been cocked with the safety on. I drop the mag, lock the slide back, and watch the extractor send the chambered round flying. I check the chamber, bolt face and mag well. Hand the empty pistol to Rincón. Pick up the loose round, snick it back into the magazine, and hand it to him. "There are six shots in there."

Rincón releases the slide, lowers the hammer, and slaps the magazine into the grip. He's not confident enough to carry a live round in the chamber. He'll be slower getting into action, but safer. I take the other pistol, do a press check, safety the weapon. Stuff it into my waistband.

"Where did you get these?" Rincón asks.

"Found them."

My room is smaller than Rincón's suite, but it's very comfortable. I open the bar and take out a bottle of wine and a bottle of Pernod. Hand out three wine glasses. "Take your pick."

Rincón and Salazar study me with suspicion. They know I didn't find the pistols. They're wondering what happened in Rincón's suite.

The matador reaches for the wine bottle. Opens it, pours himself and Salazar a glass each. I open the Pernod, pour myself a full glass. I go to the sitting area, with its coffee table, sofa and easy chairs. Collapse into one of the cushy seats. Drink, stare at the girl.

"She's trouble." I'm speaking half to myself. "One hundred and ten pounds of pure trouble."

"What do you know, Breed?" Rincón asks.

I swallow another shot of Pernod. "One group of men wants to kill her," I tell him. "They call their leader The Basque. He's a big guy with a beard. Partial to black leather car coats and 9mm Beretta 92s. That's *his* bullet in your Mercedes. His men have access to Spanish Z84 submachine guns. Also known as Spanish Uzis."

Salazar blinks.

I take another swallow. "The girl was held captive by the men in the car. Their leader is a man named Leandro. Looks like a Gypsy King, with a droopy mustache. Carries a Beretta Cheetah. Small caliber weapon. He shot The Basque in Rodilhan. I wouldn't be surprised if The Basque's leather coat stopped the bullet. Some of Leandro's men carry H&K MP5 submachine guns."

I'm not about to tell them that a Russian Spetznaz colonel wants Julia for his own reasons.

"Six men have died tonight for this girl," Rincón says.

In fact, *eight* men have died, but who's counting? I finish the Pernod, pour myself another glass.

Salazar wrings his hands. "We *must* call the police."

"The girl is afraid of the police," I tell him. "Right now, I'm inclined to trust her."

"Trust her." Rincón snorts. "She has not spoken five words all night."

"She's not a stupid girl. There's more she can tell us."

"Why does this Basque want to kill her?"

"That's what she can tell us."

Rincón paces beside the bed, looks down on the sleeping girl. "Very well," he says. "I have a suggestion."

I look at my watch. It's almost three o'clock in the morning, Easter Monday. "Tell me."

"The next *corrida* on my schedule is in Valencia. Holy Wednesday. Then we go to my ranch outside Seville. On Resurrection Sunday, I open the season at the *Maestranza*. Travel with me and the team. By the time we reach Seville, this issue will have been resolved."

"You accept the danger?"

"I accept danger every time I set foot on a *ruedo*."

"Alright." I sink deeper into the easy chair and close my eyes. Allow my hand to rest on the grip of the BM. "I'm going to get some sleep. Tell your men to stay alert. No one leaves the room tonight."

What did Orlov say?

Not now.

He might have said, "*Not yet.*"

7

ARLES – MONDAY, MORNING

"Breed," Rincón says. "Breakfast."

I jerk awake, check my watch. It's seven o'clock in the morning. A table on wheels has been rolled into the room. It's covered with a fresh white tablecloth. A buffet has been arranged on a silver service, covered to keep the food hot. Four plates and sets of cutlery have been provided.

The table has been set in the sitting area. The aroma of the meal energizes me. Salazar is seated on the sofa. Rincón stands by the closet.

Julia is sitting up in bed, her back to the headboard. Her arms are folded protectively across her chest, and she's shivering.

"Are you cold?" I ask.

"Yes."

Salazar reaches over, draws the blanket up to her chin. "There," he says. "That will keep you warm."

"We thought it best to have breakfast in the room," Rincón says. "Soon, we have to prepare to leave Arles."

I straighten in the easy chair. Distribute the plates to Salazar and Rincón. "Help yourselves." I pick up Julia's plate, put sausages and scrambled eggs on it. "Here, have some breakfast."

Julia shakes her head. "I'm not hungry," she says.

Her forehead is shiny with sweat. She twitches, pushes the blanket away. "Aren't you cold?" Rincón asks.

"Yes, but it's itchy."

Rincón shrugs, helps himself to breakfast. We exchange glances. It's clear the girl is sick.

I want to get information from the girl before she descends into withdrawal. "Julia, who's Leandro?"

Julia squirms like she's uncomfortable in her own skin. "He has my medicine."

"What medicine?"

"He gives me medicine with my food. I need it, Breed."

The girl heard Rincón call me by name. She's intelligent and alert. It's hard to tell how much of the personality she displays is Julia, and how much is Julia the heroin addict. Studies have shown that, over time, the drug literally re-wires the human brain. It wipes out some centers of cognition, reconnects others.

"We haven't any medicine for you," I tell her. "Try to eat."

"Later," Julia says.

"What were you doing in that car with Leandro?"

The girl sniffles. Her nose is running. The mucous dribbles down her chin and onto her T-shirt. Salazar hands her a cloth table napkin and she wipes her face. She closes her eyes and leans her head against the wall.

I meet Rincón's gaze and tilt my head toward the door. Together, we step into the corridor.

"It's bad," I tell him. "She was probably given her last

injection a few hours before being driven to the bar. She was entering withdrawal when we arrived at the hotel, and she is showing symptoms now. It's going to get worse."

"How long will it take for her to rid herself of this sickness?"

"The better part of a week. She has not been addicted long, and has been exposed to the drug 24/7. The withdrawal is coming upon her quickly."

"How do you know how long she has been addicted?"

"The condition of her skin. She has had numerous injections in both arms, but the track marks are fresh. Not more than a couple of weeks old. There are no signs of injections in her legs or feet. None between her fingers or toes. No scars from infected subcutaneous injections. She was forcibly addicted."

During the war on terror, forced addiction was used for enhanced interrogation. Not by Americans, because it wasn't approved. Others weren't so scrupulous. Approved or not, I wanted nothing to do with it. It was wrong, but I had another reason. Policies change. What was approved last year can land an operator in Leavenworth tomorrow.

"My God."

"The Gypsy King was holding her against her will. It takes six hours for an injection to wear off. He would have given her forced injections every six hours, day in, day out. After a week, she would be physically dependent on the drug. All he had to do was withhold it, and she would go straight into withdrawal."

"Could she really become dependent that quickly?"

I shrug. "You see the marks. Do the arithmetic. Leandro gave Julia four injections a day for seven days. That's twenty-eight injections in one week. She never came down. A recreational user taking three injections a week would require over two months to absorb the same dose. Longer to become addicted. Under Leandro's crash program, Julia developed physical dependence in as little as five days."

"Why would he do such a thing?"

"To control her. I will tell you something else—Julia is not Leandro's first victim. He refined the procedure by experimenting on many girls. Now he obtains predictable results."

"The man is a devil. And the girl's withdrawal...?"

"Will be as intense as that of a long-term addict. Leandro could not obtain her compliance otherwise."

Rincón frowns. "What do you want to do?"

"You said you have four horses for your picadors, and two horse trailers."

"Yes."

"Move all four horses into one trailer. We'll keep Julia in the other."

"We can do that."

"You have to clean it out. Two cots. One for her, one for me. Lots of blankets, pillows. Five-gallon cans of water if we can get them. Buckets to carry out anything that's been soiled. Understand. She *will* soil herself. She will soil everything."

"I understand."

"That girl is going to go through hell." I put my hands on my hips. Stare at the ceiling. "We won't get anything out of her until she comes out the other side."

Rincón digests my words. Articulating my thoughts to the matador has reinforced my conviction. Leandro kidnapped Julia to sell her into a life of prostitution. That doesn't explain Orlov's interest, or why The Basque is trying to kill her.

"Once Julia goes into withdrawal, we have to lock her in that trailer. Otherwise, she'll run. If Leandro and his crew show up, she might go back to him for a fix. Can your men be trusted?"

"Yes. All of them."

"We can't afford to be stopped by the police. They'll assume *we* kidnapped her. I won't hold you to your offer. If you want to back out, I'll stay here with the girl. Take my chances."

"You would do that for a girl you don't know."

"I reckon so."

"My God, Breed. You are a romantic. A knight in shining armor."

"I've been reading Cervantes."

"Indeed. The *corrida* is about honor. I promised to help, and I will."

"Thank you. Now—we have some arrangements to make."

JULIA MAKES it down the service elevator, supported between Salazar and Curro. We get her into the back seat of Rincón's big Mercedes 450 SEL. Curro drives us out to a barren plain on the west bank of the *Petit Rhône*. Salt water lagoons and reed-covered marshes stretch as far as the eye can see. A flamboyance of flamingoes wheels overhead and alights on the water to feed. The sun is a white hole burned into a benign blue sky.

The road sits on a low dike. The Rincón vehicles have assembled like a military convoy. Three Volkswagen Amarok pickups—two white, one cobalt blue—dominate the procession. The pickups are big, four-door vehicles, customized for

ranch use. The white pickups are hooked up to large silver
horse trailers. Boxy, with long open windows for ventilation.
The windows are high on the sides, so the horses aren't visible. All four have been moved into the last trailer.

Ahead of the horse trailers are three luxury caravans.
The one directly in front of the horse trailers is for the ranch
hands—Curro, Alvaro, and four others. The one in the
middle is for the three *banderilleros* and the two picadors.
The first caravan is for myself, Rincón, and Salazar.

Rincón's Mercedes leads the convoy, and the blue Volkswagen brings up the rear.

I won't spend much time in the caravan. Alvaro lowers
the ramp and we help Julia into the trailer. It will be her
home for the next week. Two wooden frames have been
folded against the walls. Open, they divide the trailer into
three stalls. Folded, they create a wide, comfortable space.

Two cots have been placed on opposite sides of the
trailer, close to the front. Next to one are four tin buckets.
Next to the other is a row of six five-gallon jerry cans of
water. There are stacks of blankets on the floor. Horse blankets and army surplus blankets. Garbage bags. A cloth
satchel rests at the foot of one cot.

Julia sits on the cot next to the buckets. She's drenched in
sweat. Viscous tears stream down her face and her nose
hasn't stopped running since we left the hotel. The front of
her T-shirt is soaked in mucous. She slumps onto her side,
shivering. Salazar takes off her tennis shoes and lifts her legs
onto the cot. The old man mutters prayers.

The girl gags, raises her torso, and leans out of the bed.
Salazar grabs a tin bucket and slides it next to her just in
time. She lurches to one side and vomits into the bucket. A
violent liquid stream.

Julia rolls back into bed. Her eyes are hooded. She does not bother to wipe her mouth.

"*Dios mío.*" Salazar takes a handkerchief from his pocket and dabs her lips.

Rincón picks up the cloth satchel and shows me the contents. Four lengths of white clothesline, four leather cords, and a roll of gray duct tape. If we are stopped by police, if Julia makes noise when we stop for gasoline, I might have to bind and gag her.

"It is not far from Arles to Valencia," Rincón says, "but we will take our time. Travel over secondary roads, avoid attention. We will take the long route—bypass Barcelona. Stop overnight at Castillo de Olas, arrive in Valencia on Tuesday."

"It's a plan."

"If you are right, she will go through the worst before we reach Valencia."

"I'll stay with her. She shouldn't be alone."

"There is no need for that, Breed. There are many in our party who can take turns."

I shake my head. "Let's see how it goes. Look at her. She's getting worse by the minute."

"Very well."

"Did your police contact come up with anything?"

"No. As expected, there are thousands of missing teenagers in France."

"Alright. Please watch her for a few minutes. I need to make a phone call before we leave."

I walk fifty yards along the dike. Take out my phone and hit a speed dial. It's four o'clock in the morning in Washington D.C., but Stein sounds wide awake and alert.

"Breed. You're supposed to be enjoying your bonus."

"I am. But I need your help."

"What's up?"

"I need everything you can get on Colonel Maxim Orlov, 45th Guards Spetznaz. Served in Ukraine, 2014. Fought at the Battle of Debaltseve. Later, periodically associated with PMC Wagner, but often an independent operator."

"Sounds like you already know a lot."

"That's only the first paragraph of his jacket. I met him twice. Once in Debaltseve, 2014. The second time was last night. In my hotel."

Stein gasps. "Is this a joke?"

"No joke, Stein."

I fill Stein in on the events of the last twenty-four hours. The gunfight in Rodilhan, the attack at the hotel.

"You're supposed to be on vacation, Breed."

"I didn't go looking for this. I need to know what Orlov's been up to recently. What he's working on now."

"I'll see what I can find. The Russians have been exceptionally active. Not just in Ukraine, but Turkiye and Africa."

"The Ukraine war is conventional," I say. "Not Orlov's cup of tea."

"Nor yours. Leave it with me."

"Can you use your law enforcement connections to learn about The Basque and Leandro?"

"Of course I will. How did you manage to get yourself mixed up with such a colorful cast of characters? Colonel Orlov. The Basque. And... a Gypsy King."

"You can't make this up, Stein. It *has* to be real."

"I don't doubt it."

"It all revolves around the girl. Leandro may be involved in the local drug trade. But—Julia is not a junkie."

"Are you sure?"

"Hundred percent. The needle marks are too fresh. I

reckon they've been shooting her up for a week. They're using the drug as a method of control."

"Diabolical," Stein says. "Send me a photo of the girl and I'll run it through our biometric database. If she's visited the US in the last couple of years, or has a biometric passport, we could get lucky. Now I have to go for my workout."

At four o'clock in the morning.

Stein is a machine.

8

CASTILLO DE OLAS – MONDAY, MORNING

J ulia tosses and turns on the narrow cot. Vomits. Rincón and Salazar have gone. Rincón was repelled. He was happy to see to the business of the convoy. Salazar was solicitous. Offered his help. I told him to go.

We stowed the ramp and closed the trailer gate. I was left alone with the girl.

I kick my duffel under my cot and sit down. Stare at the girl, unsure what to do.

She's sweating hard. It's like she feels hot one moment, freezing cold the next. She tears off her T-shirt and casts it aside. No bra. Her nipples are long and stiff. The aureoles are dark and large on small breasts. Her pale flesh glistens with sweat. It's a sick, feverish look. Goosebumps rise on her skin.

There's nothing I can do. The convoy sets off. The trailer sways gently from side to side. I like the sensation, but it makes Julia's nausea worse. She vomits again.

She groans. "Breed."

"Yes."

"I need medicine. Please."

My mouth is dry. "I don't have any."

Julia bends double with a violent stomach cramp. Twists into a fetal position. The buttocks of her jeans stain black. The stench of diarrhea mixes with that of vomit.

"Oh my God." She groans from pain and humiliation.

She acts drunk. Swings her legs off the cot, tries to stand.

The trailer sways and I reach to steady her. Her skin is cold and clammy. She falls back to a sitting position on the cot. Unbuttons her jeans and pulls them off. Leaves them in a puddle where they fall. Then her cotton underwear. Once white, now a uniform brown. She crawls back onto the cot.

"I'm dying," she groans.

"This will last for a while," I tell her. "You'll be fine on the other side."

Once, in Kunar, I watched a trooper go through withdrawal. We were pinned down under fire and the unit couldn't be evacuated for three days. He begged for drugs. Tried to steal syrettes of morphine from the wounded. We needed every dose, and I wanted to shoot him. Our 18-Delta —the medical sergeant—stopped me. The boy had been addicted for a long time. It took him two days to reach the state Julia finds herself in after only eighteen hours.

I pick up an empty bucket and fill it halfway with water. Pour it on Julia's naked back to rinse her off. Take an army blanket from the pile and cover her.

It's no good.

Julia can't bear the sensation of the blanket touching her skin. She rolls over, casts it aside. Lies on her back, shameless. Her stomach clenches again. Vomit and diarrhea explode from her simultaneously.

There's blood in both. She's sobbing. The skin of her belly ripples like living things are crawling inside her. I close my eyes and lean my head against the side of the trailer. Listen to the girl vomit, groan, and vomit some more. When her stomach and bowels are empty, she dry heaves.

I fall half asleep as the convoy forges its way south. I lose my sense of the passage of time.

A thud jolts me awake. I open my eyes and find Julia has rolled off her cot. Fallen onto the metal floor of the trailer.

She lifts her face to me. "Breed."

The girl's voice is a croak.

I get to my feet, try to help her back to the cot. Her skin is slippery with sweat. Naked, on her knees, she clings to my legs. "Breed. I need it. Get me something."

"There isn't any."

"Call Leandro. He has it."

"I don't know where he is. Do you know his phone number?"

That will help. With a number, Stein can geolocate him.

Julia clutches at my pants leg. "I'll do anything you want, Breed. Anything. Find him. Please. Get me some."

My God, she's fumbling with my belt.

I grasp her upper arms, pull her to her feet. "I don't know where he is."

She rubs her breasts against my chest. Tries to kiss me. "I'll do anything for you."

I jerk free. Throw her onto the cot.

Julia stares at me like a devil. Licks her lips lasciviously. "Anything, Breed. Like I did for Leandro."

Sit on my cot, stare at the girl.

Julia's voice is soft and seductive. "Anything and everything."

The next minute, she's screaming at me. "Damn you! Damn you, Breed! You are nothing! You are not even a man! I spit on you!"

I can't believe what I'm hearing. Julia rips into me with a vocabulary that would embarrass the most abusive drill instructor. Through the shock, I struggle to evaluate her accent. It's hard to place. Not German. Possibly northeast Italian? Finnish? I give up.

Julia curses me in different languages.

The girl's words echo inside my skull. I hunch over, elbows on my knees. Hold my head in my hands and shake it. Try to rid myself of her voice.

Nothing works. I can't unsee these things. Can't unhear them.

9

CASTILLO DE OLAS – MONDAY, AFTERNOON

The trailer lurches and sways to a halt. I jerk awake and find my phone buzzing. It's Rincón. "Breed, we are stopping for petrol. Come with us."

Julia lies curled into a ball, knees drawn to her chest, moaning. The girl is suffering through a fitful sleep.

I get to my feet, open the trailer gate, and lower the ramp. I step outside and breathe the fresh air. Rincón and Salazar are waiting, hands on their hips. They recoil from the stench that rolls from the interior. I close the gate behind me.

"How is she?" Rincón asks.

"She went through a difficult patch and now she's half asleep. It's not over. The vomiting and the contractions consume a great deal of energy. She is weakening. The nightmare can start again any time."

"Can she eat?" Salazar asks.

"Not a chance. It's best to keep her bowels empty. She will continue to experience vomiting and diarrhea."

I don't want Rincón to see Julia. More important, I don't

want *her* to know he saw her. I think she'll get through this. When she does, how much will she remember? I don't want her to live with the humiliation of men having seen her in that pitiful state. It can't be helped, but I want to minimize it.

The convoy has stopped on the side of the road opposite a gas station. The vehicles are taking turns pulling in to fill up their tanks. Curro and Alvaro are carrying buckets of water to the other trailer. Tending to the horses.

The rest stop looks like we could be in Kansas. The landscape is flat all around. The gas station, restaurant, and shop are a sprawling, single-story affair. I orient myself and try to catch a glimpse of ocean to the east. Nothing.

The Iberian Peninsula has plenty of mountains. Around Salamanca, and the central plateau dominated by Madrid. But the Mediterranean route, running from Arles to Perpignan and thence to Barcelona, skirts the Pyrenees.

Rincón told me we would bypass Barcelona. A shame, because I wanted to see the coast road on the way south. This trip stopped being a vacation the moment the shooting started.

I put my hand on Salazar's shoulder. "I'll clean the buckets and bring water back. Can you help wash out the floor of the trailer? Throw my duffel on the cot."

"Of course, señor."

The old man is more compassionate than Rincón. If she wakes, Julia will take to him better. I need to move around, get some air, and think.

"You must understand," I tell the old man. "The girl is not herself. She is intelligent, and she could be treacherous. She may try to seduce you. Whatever she says, don't listen to her. Don't believe her. Be kind, but do not share anything personal with her."

"What do you mean, Breed?"

"Don't talk to her about your life, your family. She'll try to use it against you. Find cracks in your armor."

"Is she *that* evil, señor?"

"No, but the drug inside her is. When it's gone, she'll be a different person."

I hope.

We work quickly. I make several trips to the gas station, a stinking bucket in each hand. Wash out the slop, carry them back empty. The clean buckets, I fill with water. Finally, I go into the gas station to do some shopping.

I find a lot of overpriced souvenir T-shirts emblazoned with *Spain, Barcelona, Valencia.* Other T-shirts with pictures of bulls on the front. I'm a bit surprised—in 2012, Catalonia banned bullfighting. But Spain is Spain, and a tourist visiting Barcelona will soon visit Seville or Madrid.

Julia's a small teenager. Five-four, maybe 110 pounds. A lot lighter now. I look for the smallest T-shirts I can find. Eyeball her size. The store has a dozen of those. I take them all, then a dozen more a size larger.

Her jeans are a problem. This is a gas station's souvenir store. I look around, find some track pants. The men's and women's are all too long. I buy three of the smallest women's and a cheap pair of scissors. When we get to the convoy, I'll cut the legs down to make her pairs of shorts.

Finally, I buy two big bottles of drinking water and plastic cups. Pay for everything with cash, carry it away in shopping bags.

When I get back to the convoy, the men are ready to leave. I open the trailer gate, step inside, and set my shopping bags on the floor.

"Breed."

Salazar tilts his head toward Julia's cot.

The girl is lying on her back, convulsing. Her back is bent into a bow, her head is thrown back, and her eyes have rolled into their sockets. She grits her teeth and groans harshly.

I show Salazar out of the trailer.

"It's alright," I say. "She'll be fine."

"*Madre de Dios. Ella esta maldita.*"

I raise the loading ramp and close the trailer gate. Sit down on my cot as the convoy pulls onto the road.

I lean my head against the wall and close my eyes.

THE NEXT HOURS plunge us back into hell. Julia dry retches until she loses her voice. Her pleas for medicine become croaks. Her curses, unintelligible growls. I tried to give her water to drink, but she slapped the cup away.

The girl has to be kept hydrated. I try again, and she accepts the cup, drains it in one swallow. Holds it out to me. Her lips move, but the word is nothing more than a raspy whisper.

I dip the cup in a bucket of water and give it to her. She drinks cup after cup, drains half the bucket. Within minutes, the terrible cramps resume. Living things crawl beneath her skin and her belly ripples. She groans. This time, the diarrhea is thin. It doesn't smell any better, but it's pure liquid.

If Julia would only sleep. Then I can sleep. The withdrawal is exhausting her frail body. The mental strain is exhausting *me*. I feel powerless, like I've lost all agency. All I can do is sit here and have my psyche beaten up. I can't think of anything else but the tortured girl in front of me. Hoping Stein has found something, I check my phone. No messages.

I'm alone.

THE CONVOY ROLLS TO A STOP. Rincón calls to tell me we've arrived at Castillo de Olas. Julia is thrashing on the cot. Her bare legs kick with the convulsions. I consider tying her down, decide against it.

I get up, stretch, and check the BM in my waistband. It's Condition One, cocked with the safety engaged. I go to the back of the trailer, open the gate, and lower the ramp. Rincón and Salazar are waiting for me. The old man starts to enter the trailer.

"No." I hold him back and raise the gate. "There's nothing we can do for her until she comes out the other side."

The air smells salty. I look around and realize we're at the seaside. The convoy has pulled off the road and parked in the shadow of a three-hundred-foot cliff. The highway runs between the cliff and the Mediterranean. The sun is low in the sky, and the cliff's shadow extends to the water.

Castillo de Olas, an eleventh century fortress, sits on the edge of the cliff. Casts its malevolent eyes on the beach and highway. It's a functional castle, built to hold this stretch of coast against marauding Moors. The structure looks intact. The east face, white at sunrise, appears tan at sunset. It rises from the cliff like it's been thrust skyward by a violent eruption deep within the earth.

The field at the base of the cliff is a lunar landscape. It slopes gently to the beach, interrupted by the paved highway and graded shoulders. The scree at the foot of the cliff consists of loose shale. This transitions into a field strewn with shrubbery and rocks of all sizes. Everything from pebbles to boulders bigger than our pickups. Some stand taller than the horse trailers and caravans. Centuries of erosion created this obstacle course. Much was ripped from the cliff during construction of the fort.

My sniper's eye detects a jagged scar that extends from the foot of the cliff to the castle. It's not a straight line. It's broken by a series of switchbacks. A trail leading from the fortress to the beach. Centuries old. There hasn't been enough modern activity around the castle to justify cutting the track into the rock.

The castle hasn't been ruined by land developers. The landscape isn't cluttered with cheap tourist shops and concessions. It's been spared because this stretch of coastline is devoid of shelter. That's why it's a *small* castle. The Moors found better places for their invasion fleets. Castillo de Olas was built at this location to guard against flanking maneuvers intended to envelop larger cities on the coast.

"We will make camp here tonight," Rincón says. "Arrive in Valencia tomorrow afternoon."

"You said we were going to skirt Barcelona. Avoid the coast highway."

"The terrain leaves us no choice." Rincón points at the castle. "Look up there."

"I see it."

"Castillo de Olas is built on a promontory. A plateau that extends west to the foothills of the Pyrenees. It forms a spur that juts toward the sea. That spur diverted the highway."

Rincón's description of the geography matches the topographical image in my mind. The Iberian Peninsula is a mass of mountain ranges, plateaus, and plains.

"You need to set watches," I tell him.

"Is that necessary?"

"The Basque and the Gypsy King know we have the girl. They know who you are, they know your schedule, they know the license number of your car. There are only a couple of routes that lead from Arles to Valencia, and they will cover both. Have you noticed any cars following us? Vehicles that showed up when we stopped?"

"No, but we have not been looking."

I've been so preoccupied with Julia, I haven't been in a position to keep a lookout myself.

"Alright. The first thing we have to do is arrange the convoy. Don't park in a column. Consolidate the vehicles into a box. The two horse trailers, their pickups, and two of the caravans should form two sides, separated by about fifty feet. The third caravan should be parked between them, in the middle. The Mercedes should close off the front of the box, and the last pickup should be parked at the back of the box."

"You are building a fort."

"That's right. It consolidates the space we have to protect. You have twelve men. Set three four-hour watches. One man at each corner of the box."

"Should we give them our weapons?"

"No, we don't have enough to go around. If you have to use yours, remember you only have six bullets."

Rincón turns to Salazar. "Make it so."

"Wait." I stop Salazar. "There's a hasp on the trailer gate. Have you got a padlock?"

"Sí, señor."

"Bring it to me, with the keys. I'm going to lock her in."

"Is she in any condition to run?" Rincón asks.

"I'm not taking any chances."

10

CASTILLO DE OLAS – MONDAY, EVENING

Julia's convulsions grow less violent. She's half asleep, twitching and whimpering. I sluice water over her naked body. Her cot and the floor under it are awash. An hour ago, I carried away the last bucket of vomit and emptied the contents under the trailer. There wasn't much. Her stomach's been empty for most of the afternoon. Her bowels too.

My phone buzzes. It's a message from Stein.

Can you talk?

At last. Maybe now I'll get some answers. I message her back.

Will call in five minutes.

I pick up two army blankets. The Spanish must buy theirs from the same supplier that makes them for the US Army. The material is soft, and I use one of the blankets to towel her dry. With the other blanket, I cover her from feet to shoulders.

Should I throw a horse blanket on top? The horse blankets are thick and rough, but warmer. I decide not to. If she gets too hot, she'll kick everything off.

I go outside and find the sun has gone down. The sky is an ocean of stars, and a full moon is rising. I close the gate and lock it. Salazar gave me a sturdy Yale padlock, big as my fist. I drop the keys in my pocket.

Stein picks up on the first ring. "How's the girl?" Stein asks.

"I think she'll be over the worst of it soon. When she comes out the other side, she'll be in terrible shape."

"I don't have anything on Orlov yet. I have a lot on Leandro and The Basque."

"Tell me."

I hear the rustle of paper. Stein's at her desk, spreading notes in front of her.

"Let's start with The Basque. His name is Armand Le Cagot. They call him El Vasco. His family was active in the separatist movement. He was involved in financing it through wholesome activities like smuggling and bank robbery. When the separatist effort faded, he carried on. Expanded into extortion, drugs, gambling and *murder*. He's more of a gangster and hit man than a freedom fighter. He's into everything dirty from Cadiz to Bilbao and Nice."

I walk out of our little compound. Allegre is standing watch at the northeast corner, facing the ocean. I nod to him and stroll to the edge of the highway. Look back on the caravan lights, the dark cliff behind the camp.

"Why is he out to kill the girl?"

"*That* is a mystery. Someone must be paying him a lot of money. The police report that his men in France and Spain are on alert."

"Is his operation big?"

"Yes. Larger in Spain than France. For whatever reason, the Spanish police can't seem to control him."

"The Basque probably bribes them. Are the French police aware of Rincón's involvement?"

"No." Stein hesitates. "I probed carefully. There was a big stink last night about the firefight in Rodilhan. Six men killed, three of them from The Basque's crew. The locals were close-mouthed. Didn't say a word about Rincón. He's an institution around there. If Rincón shot somebody, the people of Rodilhan would protect him. You and the girl left with him, so they are affording *you* the same protection."

"What about the three from Leandro's crew?"

"That's the strange part," Stein says. "They had no records. The police are frustrated and still digging."

"What did the police think of the two men I offed in the hotel?"

"They haven't found the bodies yet."

There's a full moon in the sky, and its cold light illuminates our campsite. It casts the castle, cliff and rocky field into sharp relief. Two hundred yards east, I hear the sound of waves rolling on the beach. The moon lights their foamy crests.

"What have you learned about the Gypsy King?"

I stroll slowly beside the highway to the front of the convoy. I wave casually to the ranch hand on watch at the southeast corner. He's standing by the Mercedes, smoking.

"His name is Leandro Gabarri. He has a murky past, and a murkier present."

"Gabarri. Sounds like an Italian name."

"It's Catalan. He's from Barcelona. Started life as a petty street criminal, then became an enforcer for the Spanish mafia. He was charged with killing a man. Charges were dropped. All the witnesses refused to testify. He gutted the victim with a knife."

"Nice. When I saw him, he had a Beretta Cheetah."

"That's his secondary. The knife is his preferred weapon."

"What was he doing with Julia?"

"The French police suspect Leandro of running a white slavery ring. He runs it across the south of France, through Spain, and to Morocco. The French police haven't been able to get anything on him. He's discreet. Works to order. It's clear he abducted Julia and hooked her on heroin."

"Her accent is hard to place. I'm thinking Croatian. Eastern European in any case."

"You got her talking?"

"Not exactly. She tried to convince me to give her drugs. When I wouldn't, she went berserk and screamed at me. All between convulsions and fits."

"Did her head spin around on her shoulders?"

"That's not funny, Stein."

"It was a *little* funny."

"How many men can the Gypsy King call on?"

"We don't have much intel on that. The Basque can easily call on a couple hundred soldiers from all over France and Spain. Leandro... I'm only guessing. Two dozen, maybe three. Not all will be soldiers. His operation is very different from The Basque's."

I've made a full circle around the laager. Pass the ranch hand guarding the southwest corner. He's staring at the great mass of Castillo de Olas. Bathed in the light of the full moon, it's a majestic sight.

"Thanks, Stein. I have a better idea what I'm dealing with."

"The team is still digging. I'll let you know as soon as I learn something about Orlov."

I disconnect the call. Squeeze the phone into my hip pocket, decide to make another sweep of the perimeter. I walk around the blue pickup. Say hello to Allegre on the other side.

Thumbs hooked in my belt, I thrust my hands in my pockets. The grip of the BM feels comforting. I walk past the white pickup that tows the trailer with the picadors' horses. Think about the Gypsy King. Leandro Gabarri.

Like the Spanish sun, the image of Julia offering herself to me sears my mind. *"Anything and everything, Breed. Like I did for Leandro."*

Leandro made Julia his creature. A girl willing to debase herself in every way for another needle. How could one human being do that to another? The answer must be— Leandro Gabarri is not a human being.

The door to the *cuadrilla's* caravan opens. Salazar steps out, closes it behind him. "Breed."

"Hello, Salazar."

"How is the girl?"

"Better, I think. Let us wait till tomorrow to be sure."

"I am going to sit with the maestro. Join us for a drink."

I check my watch. Julia should be safe in the trailer. "Alright."

Rincón and his manager occupy the caravan parked in the center of the laager. I cast my eye over the east perimeter. Allegre and the other ranch hand are standing at their posts. I follow Salazar between the vehicles.

The matador's caravan defines luxury. The walls are paneled with brown mahogany. There is a kitchen and a well-stocked bar. The sitting room has deep leather sofas on either side of a center table. Salazar points out that one of the sofas opens out into his bed. The floor is covered with a soft wall-to-wall carpet.

Where does the maestro sleep?

Rincón's bedroom is off-limits. It occupies the entire front of the caravan, closed off from the driver's compartment.

"Breed," the matador says. "Sit with us."

The matador is folded comfortably into a leather easy chair. It's placed at the head of the table. He's casually dressed in white trousers and a loose silk shirt, open at the chest. He's barefoot, one leg crossed over the other. He sips from a goblet of wine, gestures for us to help ourselves.

I had imagined Rincón to be a Spartan, devoted to the practice of his gladiatorial profession. No. The man is a sybarite. Was he always so? His aristocratic bearing suggests he is used to luxury.

"How is the girl?" Rincón asks.

The inevitable question. I'm tired of it. "We'll know tomorrow."

Salazar notices my annoyance. Pours wine for us. "There are two folding beds," he says. "Sleep here tonight. You look tired."

It's tempting, but there are two gangs and a Spetznaz colonel out there. I won't sleep well until this situation is resolved.

"If The Basque and his men mount a determined attack, they will overrun this camp," I tell him. "There will be time to rest when we're safe."

"When will that be, Breed?" Rincón offers us Havanas. I shake my head. Salazar takes one with thanks. Bites off the

end and lights up. Indulgent, the matador smiles. Slices
his own.

"I don't know." I finish my wine, pour another glass. "The
girl will be free of the drug by the end of the week. She may
be able to give us some answers before then."

"Yes, but is she *willing* to?"

Rincón's point is a fair one. Julia did not want the police
involved, and I don't know why. A kidnap victim would run
to the police. Her behavior suggests she has something to
fear from the police. She may not be as innocent as one
would like to think.

"I don't know. In any case, there's no reason for you to be
involved beyond the end of the week. You've put yourself in
grave danger for us. That's not fair."

"It is nothing," Rincón says. "What is life without danger?"

"What will Valencia be like?" Julia's ordeal has exhausted
me. I want to get back to my vacation, talk about bullfighting. The things that drew me to France and Spain.

Rincón gestures dismissively with his goblet. "A midweek
charity event," he says. "Little more than a warm-up for this
weekend."

"The bulls are Rafaels," Salazar says. "One of them may
surprise you. Be careful, Maestro."

Rincón's face darkens. Salazar's words remind him of the
careless slip in Rodilhan. "The world is full of surprises," he
says. "Did *that* one surprise you, Breed?"

The matador points casually. I look over my shoulder.

"No, no," Rincón says. "That scar on your neck."

I had forgotten the crease on the side of my neck. A
bullet graze from an M4 carbine, wielded by an adversary I
didn't expect.

"Yes, it did. I was lucky."

"Ah." Rincón nods his approval. "Excellent."

The matador draws out the word *excellent* with his Spanish accent. He makes it sound as though he is bestowing a golden seal of approval.

"It is better to be lucky than good, yes?" Rincón says.

We each drain another glass of wine. Salazar tops us off.

"You've got that right."

"I will show you luck," Rincón says.

The matador gets to his feet and unbuttons his shirt. Lifts the left side to reveal a horrible mass of scar tissue that runs from his navel to the top of his rib cage. "A Miura did that to me in Ronda," he says. "I have been gored fourteen times. I have scars upon scars. I do not know how many times I should have died."

"Did you kill the bull?" I ask.

"Yes, by God. They wanted to carry me to the infirmary. I stood there, bleeding, and I killed the bull."

"Bravo." I stand and unbutton my own shirt. Open it and display the entry wound of a 7.62mm AK-47 round. Half-turn, show the exit wound. "I killed the man who did that to me."

Rincón nods approval. "Truly *excellent*. Now *this*."

The matador turns around and raises his shirt. Reveals a horrible scar that stretches from the small of his back to below his right shoulder blade.

"The horn chipped my spine," he says. "From there, it entered my belly from behind. *First* the surgeons worked to ensure I would live. *Then* they struggled to ensure that I could walk."

Salazar leans forward. "The maestro is famous for standing very still while the bull brushes his *chaleco*. He will not move. He stands his ground and connects the passes into a beautiful series."

Rincón smiles. "I remain still because it is not always easy for me to move. Today, I practice the placement of the *banderillas*—to force myself to exercise agility."

I lean back, shirt open, and drain my glass. Time to switch to Pernod.

Salazar points to a scar on my belly. "What is that one, Breed?"

Absently, I look down at the small white scar. "Oh. That was a woman. With a stiletto."

"*Mucho suerte,*" Rincón says. "Women usually go after your balls."

The three of us laugh together.

11

CASTILLO DE OLAS – MONDAY, LATE EVENING

I leave Rincón's caravan before midnight. A bit unsteady on my feet, I decide to walk a circuit of the perimeter before returning to Julia's trailer. The air is fresh, and the moon is high in the sky. I breathe deeply, cross between the white pickup and the *cuadrilla's* caravan.

The east perimeter is quiet. Allegre has gone to bed, swapped duty with a ranch hand I don't recognize. On the southeast corner, another sentry paces back and forth by the Mercedes. They look awake and alert.

The sound of waves is enough to lull anyone to sleep. The moonlight glitters on the ocean, and the wave crests sparkle. There isn't a cloud in the sky—it's a field of stars.

I nod to the guard and walk around the Mercedes. Think about the scar-scape of Rincón's body. What drives a man to continue a profession that has seen him gored fourteen times? I could ask that of myself. I've stopped counting the number of wounds on my body.

The guard posted at the southwest corner is nowhere to be seen.

Annoyed, I scan the field that stretches from the camp to the base of the cliff. Has the man gone to take a piss? The moonlight casts the surface into sharp relief. The field is an obstacle course. Sandy earth, low shrubs, rocks of all sizes from loose shale to massive boulders that dwarf our caravans. Over the centuries, they've rolled down from the cliff. The son of a bitch could be anywhere.

The man shouldn't leave his post until relieved. But then, these men haven't the discipline of soldiers. Uneasy, I look north toward the other corner. I'll ask the other guard if he's seen the missing man.

Cold hands squeeze my shoulders. I can't see the guard at the northwest corner either.

My stomach tightens and I advance along the western perimeter. I pass the ranch hands' caravan. The windows are dimly lit. Faint strains of music carry from within. The sound of a man strumming a guitar. I step away from the vehicles. An attacker concealed between will have to cover more distance to reach me. My hand goes to the butt of the BM.

I walk slowly past the white pickup that tows Julia's trailer. The shadows are still. I strain my ears to hear noises Julia might be making. The windows high on the sides of the trailer are open. No sounds come from within.

My eyes continue to search the rocky field to my left. There are no signs of either watchman. Behind Julia's trailer, but between hers and that of the horses, is the blue Volkswagen pickup. My eyes search behind the windshield on the chance the watchman has decided to sit inside. Nothing.

To my right, I hear a noise. The soft crunch of a footstep on gravel. I draw the BM and thumb down the safety. Approach the corner of the trailer.

Two shadows break from behind the trailer and dash for the field of rocks. I raise the BM in an isosceles, take aim, and fire. Arms outflung, one man pitches onto his face. I switch my aim to his partner, hold my fire.

These are Leandro's crew. The Basque is more direct. Had he wanted to attack, his men would have barged into the camp with Z84 submachine guns blazing. I was able to coerce information from one of The Basque's men. If I can snag one of Leandro's, maybe I can learn Julia's story.

Cries of alarm are raised throughout the camp. I safety the BM and thrust it back in my waistband. Run after the fleeing man.

I get twenty feet, trip on a hard-soft obstacle. It's a body. Not the man I shot. One of Rincón's ranch hands. I reach for his neck to check his pulse. Withdraw my hand as though burnt. My fingers are wet from the gash in his throat.

Moonlight makes blood look black as pitch.

The camp has come alive. I can see Rincón's men silhouetted against the lights of the caravan. I hope they're not dumb enough to pursue us. The man I'm chasing is running toward the base of the cliff. I scramble to my feet and take off after him. He's hampered by an object he carries in his right hand. It's two feet long and heavy. A tool of some kind.

We stumble along the rocky field. It's slow going. Let's say we're not sprinting. That would be a good way to turn an ankle, or worse. No, we're jogging, careful not to trip. Maintaining balance over this obstacle course is physically exhausting. The man looks back every few yards, checks to see if I'm gaining on him. I am. Looking back is costing him ground. Within a few seconds, I'll be in striking distance. I gather myself for a tackle.

The man runs past a massive boulder. Bigger than Julia's

trailer. I'm about to launch myself at him when I'm hit from the side. A large form separates from the mass of the boulder, slams into me with brute force.

Bushwhacked. How could I have thought there were only two intruders? *Of course* they had confederates waiting in the field. I'm knocked to the ground. There are three men coming from behind the boulder.

I land heavily on my side. The man who charged skips over me. I claw for the BM, raise it one-handed toward the two others swarming from the boulder. The man I was chasing turns and swings the tool he's carrying. It's a bolt cutter. He uses it like a club, brings it down hard on the muzzle of the BM.

I fire, but the blow spoils my aim. Knocks the pistol from my hand. The muzzle flash illuminates my attackers and the bullet whines off rock. In the glare of the muzzle flash, I recognize Leandro's dark features and drooping mustache. In his hand, the moonlight glints off a curved, eight-inch blade.

The man with the bolt cutter loses his balance. I grab his arm, lock and break it at the elbow. He screams and I force him onto his face. Leandro swings his blade in a wide arc. I jerk backward, feel the blade slash my left shoulder.

The man who barged into me has gotten between me and the camp. Draws his own blade. The man with Leandro comes around him so he has a clear path. It's four-on-one, and all my opponents are armed. The man with the broken arm is pressing it to his chest to immobilize it. He's drawn a knife with his left hand.

I don't care how well trained a man is. Four-on-one, where the four have knives and the one doesn't, is a losing game. The one is going to die. You don't go one-on-one against a knife without getting cut. That's the first thing they teach you in combatives. There are no supermen. Men like that only exist in movies and dime store novels. You don't get *cut* once. You get cut twenty times. You don't get *stabbed* once. You get stabbed thirty times. They don't stand back and admire their work. Like, *Oh, that was a great cut. I'm such an artiste.* No. They fillet you, they stab you to death.

Somewhere on Leandro's person is a seven-round .380 caliber Cheetah.

He who hesitates is lost. I'm not going hand-to-hand against four knives and a pistol. There's only one way out. I turn and run for the cliff.

"*¡Mátalo!*"

The field is a fucking obstacle course. Thank God for the moonlight. Once your eyes adjust, the light of a full moon is almost as good as daylight. I run hard, lifting my knees high, jinking around obstacles. I stumble, fall, jump to my feet, keep going. There are cries and curses from behind.

I look back. Leandro and his bunch aren't in the best of shape, and I'm pulling away from them. The man with a broken arm is falling behind. Is there a way I can break contact and make my way back to the camp? I don't think so. If I run to either side, they'll have a chance to close the distance and cut me off.

The gypsies have an efficient stride. I'll give them that. They're running with knives in their hands. I wouldn't risk falling on one of those blades. Can't imagine those blades were made for any legitimate purpose.

Keep running. The cliff is blocking my way. It's going to force me left or right anyway. Unless I find a way to climb.

I hit the scree and scramble over the loose shale. I remember the goat trail carved into the side of the cliff.

Where is it? I have to find it. Start climbing before they catch me.

The path has at least three switchbacks, I recall. To make it easier to climb. It has to start off to one side of the base, but not too far. I cast about for a likely spot, but nothing leaps out. The moonlight slashes the cliff face into a craggy mass of jagged shadows. It's impossible to tell where the trail begins.

I'm sucking wind as I run along the base of the cliff. I can hear the gypsies gasping behind me. That means they're gaining. Rushing to cut me off. I look back. Shit, most of the lead I built up has gone. They're only fifteen or twenty yards back. I look left. Stumble, reach out with my left hand and push off the cliff face to keep my balance. That's how sheer the face is, that's how close we are to the wall.

Stumble again. Reach out, find nothing to lean on, fall over. I cry out as pain burns through my cut shoulder. One man, faster than the others, is upon me. I lash out with my foot, connect with his knee.

"*¡Aiee—coño!*"

The man pitches forward, falls across me. His blade scrapes the stone. I roll over, try to kick his head off. Make contact, but can't generate enough force to knock him out.

Get to my feet. I've found the foot of the goat trail by accident. Of course, it would have to be an indentation in the wall. Leandro lunges for me. I dance out of the way, grit my teeth, and sprint up the trail. First rule of hill running. Drive your arms, and your knees will lift.

I don't bother to look back. Just run like hell. The exertion burns my quads. Fine. If they turn to lead, I'll be in trouble. It's three hundred feet up. The switchbacks make the distance longer, but allow you to climb faster.

Hit the first switchback. It's like the goat trail narrows, then comes to a dead end. I find myself staring into space, then a hundred feet straight down. I'm gasping. Spit, only to have it land on my heaving chest. Turn right, support myself with both hands on the wall. Find the trail widening on the other side of the switchback.

Leandro is ten yards back, wheezing. His legs are wobbly, and he's leaning against the face with the fist of his knife hand. Two men are right behind him. The man with the broken arm is nowhere to be seen.

I suck a deep breath, then sprint up the next switchback. Again, I refuse to look behind me. Leandro's breath has become a high-pitched whine. His men are breathing hard too, and none of them are in sync.

If I'm hurting, they're dying. The next switchback is worse than the last. Now I'm staring into a chasm two hundred feet deep. I ignore it, turn, and keep pumping. My legs are turning into sticks of wood.

There's a sharp crack. Next to me, a bullet strikes sparks from stone. Rock chips sting my face. I ignore the pain, keep going. Hit the top, turn and look back.

Leandro's fallen to his knees twenty yards back, unable to go on. Knew he wasn't going to catch me before I reached the top, drew his pistol and fired. His two men, in better shape, clamber past him and keep coming. Leandro stuffs the pistol into his waistband, retrieves his knife, and struggles to his feet.

The goat trail opens onto a narrow shelf. There, the cliff face transitions into the castle's east wall. I look up. The wall is another sixty feet high, topped with stone crenellations. Flush to the center is a twenty-foot high keep. I wouldn't want to have been a Moorish soldier storming Castillo de Olas.

Now I have the same problem as before. If I run back and forth along the base of the castle wall, Leandro and his crew will have time to catch up. It's not like the castle's architects would have made a gate in the east wall just for good old Breed. Their job was to keep Moors out, not let them in.

I have to buy time. Cast around for a weapon. Anything. There, big and black in the frigid moonlight. An oblong piece of rock twice the size of a bowling ball. I get my hands around its jagged edges. Bend my knees and lift it over my head. It must weigh sixty pounds.

Poke my head around the corner. The three gypsies are charging up the path, sweating and swearing. Leandro is bringing up the rear. Six or seven yards separate me from the first man.

Hill running is wonderful. When you're sucking wind, you don't look up. You're dying, and you don't think further than your next step. That's what these men are doing right now. They're thinking, *One more step, one more step, get to the top.*

I hurl the rock at the first man with all my strength. With luck I can take all three of them out.

There's a dull whack as the rock connects with the crown of the man's head. He makes no sound. Drops his knife, staggers, and falls against the man behind him. The second man is taken by surprise. Tries to support his friend, but the first man is unconscious, a sack of dead weight, already pitching sideways. The number two man is too exhausted to keep him from falling.

Without a sound, the man topples into space.

The three of us watch him fall. The trail has been doubling back on itself, cutting deeper into the rock face with every switchback. The body hits the trail at the level of the second switchback like a limp rag doll. Bounces with a sickening *thwack*, plunges another hundred feet, and hits the first level with a wet crunch. It cartwheels the final hundred feet and disappears into the blackness. I can't hear the final impact.

Leandro and the other man glare at me, their faces silver in the moonlight.

"*¡Bastardo!*"

Well, pardon me for wanting to live.

I cast about for another rock, but Leandro's drawn his pistol again. Raises it with an unsteady hand and fires. *Pop, pop, pop.* Three muzzle flashes sparkle from the small caliber weapon. Bullets whine off stone.

Time to displace. I turn and run hard along the base of the castle wall. Reach the end, turn the corner, keep going. A foolish thought crosses my mind. Two down, two to go. I think of Leandro hooking Julia on heroin. Doing things to her. I want him under my knife. I want to make him tell me everything—where she came from, how he took her. Then I'll kill him.

Suicidal. I'm still facing a pistol and two knives.

My left shoulder is hot and sticky. The left sleeve of my shirt is soaked in blood.

On the right, I see an arched gateway. It's a side entrance, an opening in the castle wall. A millennium ago, it was protected by an iron portcullis. Murder holes in the wall above. Today it yawns wide.

I can continue to run straight along the wall, or I can go inside.

Beyond the castle, bathed in moonlight, are the ruins of a

medieval stone village. Little remains but rubble and low walls. They stretch across three hundred yards of the plateau. Like any modern military post, the castle garrison would have been served by a local civilian population. They would defend against attack from the beach below. If, by chance, the enemy occupied the plateau around the castle, the villagers would shelter behind the castle walls.

There must be another way off the plateau. The village would be supplied over roads from the west. That's no good. I want to get back to the Rincón caravan. That means I have to either go back down the goat trail or find another path.

Rincón told me Castillo de Olas was built on a spur that jutted toward the ocean. That means there must be slopes to the north and south as well as the west. The only question is, how steep are they?

I'm not about to run around the edge of the plateau looking for a way down. Not with two bloodthirsty gypsies out to get me.

On the other hand, I'm as bloodthirsty as they are. Maybe more so. If I can kill Leandro's last man, it's down to one-on-one. I don't care that he's got a knife and a gun. Man-to-man, I can take him. I'll find a way to tilt the field in my favor.

I decide to keep my options open. Dodge through the arched gateway, glance around. The crenellated keep rises high over the east wall. That's the narrowest section of the fortification. It overlooks the cliff.

If I can channel their approach through a narrow passage, I can tackle them one at a time. The gateway is too wide for that.

The castle forms a wider, oblong enclosure on the plateau. It might be a hundred yards long on each side and a hundred and fifty yards wide where it borders the village. The crenellations and murder holes circle the walls. In addition to the keep, there are towers at each of the fort's four corners.

I know the stairways inside the towers will spiral upward in a clockwise direction. That causes right-handed attackers to have difficulty swinging their swords. Ditto gypsies wielding knives. If all Leandro and his friend had were knives, I'd place myself at the top of a staircase and pick them off.

Leandro, of course, has a pistol.

In that respect, Leandro's Cheetah affects the calculation.

I hear running footsteps crunching on gravel. The main gate is another arched portal in the west wall. Like the one to the south, it's missing a portcullis. I'm not about to play hide and seek with Leandro and his man in the castle. I run for the gate.

Fifteen seconds, and I'm through the west gate. I jog toward the ruins of the village as the gypsies come through the opening in the south wall. It's not a big village, and there's no place to hide. There isn't a wall standing more than three feet high. In a gunfight, these ruins would make good cover, but I'm not looking at a two-way shooting gallery. This shooting gallery works one-way, and I'm the target.

I have to make sure I'm not a sitting duck.

I've got my second wind, and I run to the south edge of the plateau. Leandro and his man run toward me. I look down the slope. It's not a cliff. We're still three hundred feet above the beach level, and it's a steep slope. Defenders on the castle walls could fire down on attackers struggling to climb to the plateau.

A steep slope, and a challenge to attackers storming the

castle. But not so steep as to require a switchbacked goat trail. I think I can run down if only I can keep my balance.

With the gypsies pounding after me, I take a breath and start the descent. The slope is mostly loose shale, not boulders and broken rock like mountain slopes I saw in Afghanistan. I take a few steps to test the consistency of the surface. This tentative pace won't do. The gypsies will be on me in a minute. Leandro will try to pick me off. I start to lope down the hill.

I hear cries behind me. Loose shale clatters and rolling rocks overtake me as the gypsies give chase. Heart pounding, I lean forward and run. Gravity takes over, and my legs start to turn. Second rule of hill running—lean forward, but not so far that you lose control.

Another *pop* and a bullet passes me in the dark. Leandro is exhausted, and he's firing on the run. He's got two rounds left. Three if he kept one in the chamber.

The gypsies are swearing. I see a cluster of boulders and swerve around them. The course change gives me a better line. I lean back, fall on my ass, and slide ten yards before I find my feet and continue to run.

I hit the flats at speed, turn toward the ocean, and burst into an all-out sprint. I cast a glance back and see the gypsies reach the bottom of the slope. They give chase, but I'm in better shape. The highway's in sight, and the lights of the caravans burn less than two hundred yards away.

From behind a boulder, a figure springs into my path. It's the gypsy with the broken arm. He's got it tucked into the front of his shirt like a makeshift sling. A curved blade shines in his left hand.

This is no contest, but dispatching the cripple slows me up. He thrusts low with the knife. I grab his wrist, lock it, and twist the knife out of his hand. Put him down, but the other gypsy and Leandro are catching up to me.

Leandro's older and in worse shape. The other gypsy reaches me first, stabs downward with his knife. When he attacks, I'm bent low over the man with the broken arm. I deflect the blow with my left forearm and get under the attacker. Hit him at the level of his knees, straighten my legs, and thrust forward and up.

With a cry, the man sails over my head and does a face-plant on the rocks. In a heartbeat, I rise to face Leandro—who is already running.

A shot rings out from the direction of the camp. Voices shout in Spanish. The three gypsies run like the devil himself is after them.

I get to my feet and dust myself off. Leandro and his men are running south, losing themselves in the moonscape of rocks, shrubbery and boulders. Rincón, Salazar, Allegre and another of Rincón's *cuadrilla* are running toward me. Rincón has a BM in his hand.

Allegre starts to run after the gypsies.

"No," I say. "Leandro has a gun."

Salazar takes my hand, straightens my arm. "You are wounded, Breed."

Adrenaline and the sting of battle tend to kill pain. I'm coming down from the rush of combat and my shoulder is starting to burn. "Yes. It didn't slow me down much."

"Come, I will see to it."

"They were trying to break into the girl's trailer when I interrupted them."

"The girl is fine," Rincón says. "They did not get inside."

12

CASTILLO DE OLAS – TUESDAY, EARLY MORNING

I insist on looking in on Julia. Rincón was right—the padlock is intact. I remove it and we step inside. Julia's tossing and turning. Groaning with cramps. The violence of the convulsions, however, is not as severe as it was in the afternoon.

We leave the girl alone and replace the lock. Salazar takes me into Rincón's caravan. My shirt is a write-off. I strip to the waist and examine the wound. The old man wipes off coagulated blood with a wet towel. That's great, the wound starts bleeding again. It's a superficial cut, six inches long. Extends from the lower point of my deltoid and scythes to my elbow. The lips of the wound open to reveal red flesh underneath.

"Another war story, eh, *hombre*?"

The manager opens a small refrigerator in the living space. Inside is a box packed with vials of morphine. An adjacent cabinet is filled with boxes of plastic syringes. He tears open the cellophane container of a disposable syringe with his teeth. Injects me with the painkiller. Finally, he swabs my cut with antiseptic and sews it up with a minor surgery kit.

"You're well equipped," I observe.

"One has to be. Maestro has been gored many times. The medics at the infirmaries of the bullrings are very capable, and so are those at local hospitals. But once we are on the road between events, I am left to manage Maestro's wounds."

Salazar closes the tin container and stows it. Opens the refrigerator once more and hands me a cardboard box. "Penicillin," he says. "I assume you are not allergic."

"No, I'm not."

"Good. There is enough for a ten-day course. You must not miss any doses."

The manager disappears into Rincón's bedroom, comes back with a cotton shirt and hands it to me. "You and the maestro are the same size," he says.

"I have a change of clothes in my duffel."

"You may borrow it. The maestro will not mind."

Rincón opens the door, steps inside. "We have located the body of our second watchman," he says. "We have found three bodies. Two of my men, killed with knives. One man, you shot."

"There is another at the foot of the cliff," I tell him. "We should collect him in the morning."

"We can get him now."

"No," I say. "Keep the men close to camp. There's no guarantee Leandro and his men have gone."

"Very well," Rincón says. "But we cannot leave the bodies exposed. Neither can we take them with us."

"What do you want to do?"

"We will bury them here. Otherwise, griffon vultures will pick them clean. Worse, the vultures will expose their location to curious eyes."

"I don't care about Leandro's men," I tell him, "but what will you say to the families of your men?"

"Don't worry," the matador says. "We will come back for the bodies when it is safe to do so. I will take care of their families. They are loyal."

"Alright. Keep a sharp lookout. Remember those killers managed to sneak up on us."

"I doubt anyone will sleep for the remainder of the night."

"Breed," Salazar says, "*you* must sleep."

"I think I will. After I recover my gun."

"Sleep in our caravan. I will stand at the gate of the girl's trailer until you awake."

Salazar walks with me to the boulder where Leandro and his men ambushed me. I switch on the flashlight in my phone and search the area. The BM lies exactly where I dropped it. Two feet away is the heavy bolt cutter used to knock the weapon from my grasp.

I pick up the pistol and lower the hammer. I give Salazar my phone and have him hold the flashlight. Drop the magazine, rack the slide, and catch the ejected bullet. Then I snick the loose round back into the magazine.

Next, I examine the barrel and do a three-point safety check. Mag well, bolt face, chamber. I rack the slide and dry fire the weapon. Finally, I insert the magazine, draw the slide back and let go. The slide chambers a round with a satisfying clack. I engage the safety and tuck the weapon under my shirt.

I take the phone back from Salazar, turn the flashlight off. "They've been watching us," I tell him.

"How can you be sure?"

"They knew to bring the bolt cutter."

13

CASTILLO DE OLAS – TUESDAY, MORNING

Griffon vultures circle the base of the cliff two hundred yards south of our camp. We recovered the body of the man I knocked off the goat trail. His skull was crushed and his body was like a sack of loose bones. It squished as we carried it back to camp and put it with the others.

"Bury" doesn't accurately describe the process. We laid the bodies in a row behind a group of large boulders. Then we piled rocks over them until we had four mounds.

Now we stare at the vultures. Big scavengers with eight-foot wingspans.

"Have we missed something?" Rincón asks.

"I only killed two men."

"Let us go and see."

Salazar organizes the convoy for departure while Rincón and I investigate the carrion. It's a body in torn clothing lying on the rocks. Vultures stand around, tearing meat from the corpse. Others circle overhead, waiting for an opportunity to swoop down for a bite. The birds have bodies four feet long, head to tail. The birds' heads, normally white, are stained red from being dipped in the corpse's blood.

I'm not about to waste a bullet to drive them off. Rincón and I stoop, pick up rocks, and hurl them at the scavengers. Walk over and examine their meal.

A white skull's face leers up at us. The vultures have ripped the eyes from their sockets, the lips and tongue from the mouth. It's the man whose arm I broke. His hands have been bound with his belt.

"What killed him?" Rincón asks.

I point to a hole in the skull between the eye sockets. "That's what's called a thirty-five-cent solution."

"Why would Leandro kill his own man?"

"I'm not sure he did. This poor guy couldn't keep up. Someone else was out here last night, picked him off."

"Why?"

"His hands are bound. I can't tell what's been done to him because the vultures have been busy destroying evidence. It's a good bet he was tortured for information."

"Who would do that?"

I haven't told Rincón about Orlov. I don't know that the Russian colonel was responsible for this atrocity, but neither do I know that he wasn't. The Basque could have done this, but it's not his style. Armand Le Cagot is a blunt instrument. Had he been out here last night, he and his men would have come at us with guns blazing.

"The Basque. Remember there are two groups out there interested in Julia."

Rincón shakes his head. "It makes no sense."

"Not yet, but I know one thing."

"What is that?"

"We need help, and we can't go to the police."

I start piling rocks on the body. "Help me cover him up. We should hit the road."

Together, we pile stones on the dead man. When we are finished, we walk back to the convoy. Behind us, we leave another funeral mound.

I GO BACK inside Julia's trailer. She's sleeping, her movements much less spastic. Softly, she whimpers.

Sitting on my cot, I take out the track pants I bought her and cut the legs down to the length of baggy shorts. I haven't the time or patience to hem the shorts, so I leave them as they are. Salazar promised to launder her jeans, T-shirt and underwear. They'll be dry tomorrow. When she wakes, I'll give her a pair of shorts and one of the souvenir T-shirts I bought.

The Basque is a problem. Leandro's men have weapons, but seem to prefer knives. Had they arrived with submachine guns last night, I wouldn't have had a chance. When Armand Le Cagot finds us, his men will lay waste to everything in sight.

I need help. Take my phone out and message Stein. *Can you talk?*

The phone buzzes almost as soon as the check marks indicate she's read my message. "Breed, what's up?"

"The Gypsy King made a move on the girl last night. Killed two of Rincón's men. I killed two of theirs, wounded one. They ran off. This morning, we found the wounded man murdered. I think Orlov did it."

"Why?"

"I think he wanted to know more about Leandro's operation. We're being shadowed by Leandro's men. I've been preoccupied with the girl. Haven't been in a position to keep watch. Rincón's men are amateurs. I need help."

"What kind of help?"

"Professional help. Operators who can be relied upon for both offensive action and executive protection. I need two men. Takigawa if you can get him. One more. You know the type."

"Yes. Walking death machines."

"We were lucky last night. If attacked in force, this convoy is indefensible. Rincón and I have two pistols and thirteen rounds between us."

"I'll see what I can do."

"There's more."

"Tell me."

"I can't stay cooped up with this teenaged kid. I need freedom of movement so I can keep watch and engage the enemy at will. At the same time, I can't keep her locked up. She's coming out the other side. When she does, she'll object. And I want her to be able to talk to someone she can relate to."

"Go on."

"I'm going to ask Heth Crockett for help."

"Do you think she will?"

"I think she'll do it for me."

"You think so, do you?"

"Yes. If she agrees, I need you to fly her to Spain. Ideally, she and Takigawa will arrive together."

Stein is silent for a full three beats. "Alright. I'll talk to Takigawa, you talk to Heth."

We sign off, and I call Rincón. "What's the plan for today?"

"We drive," the matador says. "We should arrive in

Cheste by late afternoon. It is in the Valencia community. Tomorrow it will host a charity *corrida*. We will camp in a field outside, drive into town for the event."

"You'll take the horses?"

"Yes. It would be best if you and the girl remained in camp. I do not expect the *corrida* to be eventful."

"Alright. I would like to stop in the first town we encounter. I need to do some shopping."

"There is a town half an hour away. We can stop there."

"Thank you."

I disconnect the call. Lean back, and think of Heth Crockett. It's one o'clock in the morning back in Montana. That gives me five hours to figure out what to say.

14

VALENCIA – TUESDAY, MORNING

The wheels of the trailer thrum on the well-maintained Spanish highway. After stopping for an hour in a roadside town, the convoy is making its way to Valencia. I took my shopping list into a series of shops while Rincón and his men ate a late breakfast. Carried my goods back to the trailer. I had to make two trips.

Julia lifts her head. "What are you doing, Breed?"

I've moved my cot to the back, next to the gate. Set the items I bought on the floor. "Cooking. Are you hungry?"

"No." The girl stretches out on the cot. Rests her head on one arm, closes her eyes. "I want to sleep. Maybe I will eat later."

It's the first time I've seen Julia stretch her thin body. For the last thirty hours, she's either been convulsing or lying curled up in a ball. Her voice is hoarse, but her words have lost the feverish desperation of withdrawal.

"Okay," I tell her. "I bought us some sandwiches. Let me know when you want to eat."

No answer. The girl is sound asleep.

I turn back to my cooking. I bought a plastic child's bathtub in town. A foot deep, and big enough to contain two of the tin buckets. I set four quart-sized plastic bottles of drain opener on the floor next to me. Two different brands. The labels are in Spanish, but fortunately, the symbols representing their chemical ingredients are common to most western languages. The two brands are made with different household acids in different concentrations.

On my right are six glass perfume bottles purchased in the beauty section of the town drugstore. The bottles are each standard twelve-ounce volumes. I emptied the contents onto the side of the road before we left. The ranch hand driving the blue pickup stared at me with a puzzled expression on his face. Next to the empty perfume bottles is a large plastic container of vegetable glycerine. It's a standard bakery ingredient available at the supermarket. None of the items I purchased raised an eyebrow.

Behind me are two jerry cans of water. At the gas station, I bought large plastic bags of ice. Next to the tin buckets lies a foot-long ceramic stir stick, also purchased at the supermarket.

I pour water from one of the jerry cans into the bathtub until it's half full. Then I empty a plastic bag of ice into the tub. Finally, I set one of the tin buckets in the water. I square myself in front of the tub and make myself comfortable. Tie a handkerchief over my nose and mouth.

Carefully, I mix the two different brands of drain opener in the tin bucket. They have to be mixed in a certain ratio. I stir the contents gently, and the bucket grows hot from the chemical reaction.

I wait for the bucket to cool, then carefully decant the mixed acid into the empty plastic bottles. Keep them separate from the others I haven't opened. I bought twice as much as I needed in case it became necessary to repeat the exercise. Next, I rinse the bucket and pour the rinse water into the other empty bucket.

The ice has melted. I pour some of the water out, and dump another bag full of ice into the tub. Then I set the empty bucket back in the tub. Open the container of vegetable glycerine, pour half of it into the bucket.

Here we go. I deliberately selected the concentrations of drain opener so the chemicals would not be too reactive. That makes the process easier to control. I shake out my arms to loosen them up. Take a bottle of acid in one hand and the ceramic stir stick in the other. Slowly, I pour the acid into the glycerine. Stir the mixture. In a lab, I'd have the benefit of an electromagnetic stirring device to maintain a smooth mixing action. In the field, we make do.

I've done this before, so I know what to expect. Minutes pass, and a thin plume of smoke issues from the surface of the liquid. I stop pouring, continue to stir. Wait for the smoke to disappear. It rises toward the roof of the trailer, drifts out the high windows. When the smoke is gone, I resume pouring. Several times over the next thirty minutes, I have to stop to give the fumes time to clear.

The smell of acid grows sharp in the closed space. The open windows are too high to clear the fumes. The chemical reaction is turning the liquid into vapor at a steady rate. The conversion occurs at the liquid-to-air interface. This is how states of matter change. In a lab, I'd have a fume hood. In the field, I keep a cloth tied over my nose and mouth.

I empty one of the two bottles of acid. Set it aside, open the other, start pouring. Pour and stir, pour and stir. Be patient, Breed. Slow is fast. This is where impatient operators can have a bad day. Sometimes it's the last day of their lives.

When the second bottle has been thoroughly mixed in, I have a bucket full of liquid explosive. I picked the ingredients carefully. Mixed them in ratios to create a compound more stable than nitroglycerine.

This explosive can be set off with a detonator, but it can also be set off by high temperatures, or by physical shock. When eyeballing the ratios, I erred on the side of stability. I didn't want to blow up the horse trailer at the first bump in the road. It will take a more violent shock, like a car crash, to detonate the bucket.

I take the glass perfume bottles, fill each to the brim, and seal them.

There's a little of the explosive left at the bottom of the bucket. I take one of my pillows and cut it open with scissors. Shake the stuffing into the bucket and use it to soak up what's left of the liquid. The stuffing, saturated with explosive, won't blow up on impact. Detonating the stuffing requires a blasting cap or a makeshift detonator.

It's a kind of dynamite.

I know how to make detonators. The good thing about Special Forces is the cross-training one gets from other specialists on the teams. I was trained as a weapons specialist, but spent a lot of time with 18-Charlies. The Charlies are the engineer sergeants. They are specialists in building and demolitions. Delta Force breachers are often 18-Charlies. They are taught to make improvised explosive devices from common household items.

One good thing about the environmentalist movement is the return to paper drinking straws. I can take a paper drinking straw, fill it with gunpowder, and stick it in the explosive-soaked stuffing. Where do I get gunpowder? Buy a mortar and pestle at a store that specializes in natural organic shit. They are so trendy these days. Grind up a little salt, charcoal and sulfur in the proper ratio. There you go.

I'll keep the dynamite for later, in case I need it. My current task and purpose does not require fused explosives.

I move my cot back to the front of the trailer, opposite Julia. Scoop the dynamite into a plastic bag and seal it with a knot. I put the bag and all my materials away under my cot. Shove my duffel into place next to them. Everything looks innocent. I use water from the jerry cans to rinse out the tin buckets.

Finally, I take one bucket, pour three inches of water into it, and set the six twelve-ounce perfume bottles inside. Shake ice from a plastic bag into the bucket and pack it tight. The explosive shouldn't detonate at room temperature, but I'd rather not take chances. I set the bucket at the foot of my cot. Take the plastic bathtub, turn it over, and cover the bucket.

I now have six improvised hand grenades.

15

VALENCIA – TUESDAY, NOON

The convoy stops for lunch at another rest area. I make sure to lock Julia's trailer. Take my phone and charger, go into the restaurant. Rincón and his men occupy a long table at the back. The matador waves me over.

I gesture to my phone. Indicate I need to make a call. Find an isolated table and plug my charger and universal adapter into the wall socket. Search my contacts, find Heth Crockett's number. Thumb hovering over the entry, I hesitate. Take a deep breath, make the call.

Pray she's not in the woods. Mobile phone reception in Montana can be spotty. If she's home at the Crockett Ranch, we'll be fine.

Heth picks up on the third ring. Her tone is mildly annoyed. "Breed. This is a surprise."

"Spain is ranch country," I say. "I was thinking about you."

Twenty-five years old, nubile, and more than ready, Heth has been crushing on me since she was sixteen. Made no secret of it. Her grandfather was my father's best friend during the Vietnam war. Members of the elite MACV-SOG, they ran special operations into Laos when America wasn't supposed to be there. I always knew Sam Crockett wanted me for Heth. Before he died, he came right out and told me so.

"No, you weren't."

Heth and I engage in friendly flirtation all the time. She usually throws herself at me and expects me to fight her off. If we ever act on the mutual attraction, the sex would blow our heads off. But our relationship would never be the same.

Neither of us is ready for that.

"I was, too. How would you like to join me in Spain for my vacation?"

"What's the catch?"

"I need your help to wrap up some business. It'll only take a few days."

Heth sounds suspicious. "I knew it. What kind of business?"

"The kind only you can help me with. I have to take care of a runaway girl for a few days. Until we find her family and send her back."

"Who is she?"

"That's the problem. We don't know. She was kidnapped by some very bad people. They hooked her on drugs and I took her away from them. She's off the drugs now, but she's still very weak." Inspiration strikes. "*She needs a friend.*"

Heth's a nice girl with a good heart. But she's not stupid. "These bad people you took her from. I bet they're still after her."

I swallow. "Yes, they are. In fact, there are a number of

bad actors after her. But I'll take care of them. I'm getting help. Ken Takigawa and another operator."

"How do I get there?"

"Stein's going to arrange everything. She'll probably put you all on the same military flight, top priority."

"*That* witch? Is *she* going to be there?"

I cringe. Stein and Heth do *not* get along. Stein may be nerdy, political, and ambitious as hell, but she *is* attractive. The jealousy between the two women is palpable.

"No, she's not. She's just doing me a favor."

I hear the sound of Heth cracking open a beer can. All of a sudden, I'm thirsty. Rincón, Salazar and the men are conversing at their table. There's a line forming at the buffet. I find myself wanting food and a drink.

Heth adopts a demanding tone. "Tell me about this vacation."

I hear, *Convince me.*

"Tonight we're going to Valencia. I'm travelling with the best bullfighter in the world. It's Holy Week, and tomorrow he's performing at a *corrida* for charity. After that, we go to his ranch in Andalusia."

Heth's ears prick up. "He has a *ranch*?"

Aha, I've found a hook. "Not only does he have a ranch, he raises fighting bulls."

"Will I get to see them?"

"That's the plan. I need you and Takigawa here *before* we get to the ranch."

"Will I get to see what's-his-name... perform?"

"Javier Rincón. I think that can be arranged. On Resurrection Sunday, he'll be the number one matador at the *Maestranza.* Seville's bullring."

"I'll do it," Heth says. "On one condition."

"What's that?"

"I want him to teach me how to bullfight."

"What's that?"

Heth takes a long pull of her beer. Cracks open another can. "That's the deal. I'm tired of weak-ass barrel racing. I can ride, shoot and fuck. Now I want to bullfight."

16

VALENCIA – TUESDAY, EARLY EVENING

I say goodbye to Heth and exhale through puffed cheeks. Put my phone away, get up and go to the buffet. I buy myself a sandwich and two cans of beer. Join Rincón at his table. Salazar and the other men share somber expressions. These men are used to hard, dangerous work, but not the direct violence that we experienced last night.

"Breed," he says. "Give us the news."

"I have called for help," I tell him. "I expect friends to join us on the road. Julia's condition is improving. By the end of the week, we will leave you and your people in peace. With thanks."

His expression grave, Rincón nods. "Yes. I have great concern about these men who stalk us."

"The Basque is most dangerous," I say. "Leandro wants to kidnap the girl, The Basque wants to kill her."

"But *why*?"

"When we know *that*, we'll know everything."

Rincón throws up his hands. "When will the girl be able to speak?"

"Soon, but she is very weak. The withdrawal sapped her strength. I hope she will be able to eat and drink tonight."

We sit in silence while I eat my sandwich and drink my beers. Allegre and several of the men get up to see to their vehicles.

"There is something we should do." I look from Rincón to Salazar and back. "We should change the order of our vehicles at every stop."

"Why?"

"We're being watched. Certainly by Leandro. Probably by The Basque as well. Leandro knew we put a padlock on the gate of Julia's trailer. That's why they brought the bolt cutter. The Basque knew Leandro was making a move on us last night. He stood back because he didn't want a bloodbath like the one in Rodilhan. But afterward, he snatched the man with the broken arm."

In truth, I don't think The Basque killed the man with the broken arm. I think Orlov did it. But I have to pitch The Basque to Rincón. Otherwise, he'll know a third party is involved and won't quit until I tell him who that is.

"Let's play a shell game with the girl," I say. "There are only two trailers, so we'll switch them up on the road. When we bivouac, we'll switch up their positions in the laager. When the girl is stronger, she won't need to ride in a trailer."

"You make good sense, my friend," Rincón says. "Very well. Let me know when your friends are going to join us."

THE BARE BULB on the ceiling of the trailer sways rhythmically. The convoy continues south. The roads are smooth, the traffic light. I lie face-up on my cot, phone to my ear. Julia sleeps peacefully. She's come through.

"Morón Air Base," Stein says.

"Never heard of it."

"It's a joint Spanish-American base thirty-five miles outside Seville. We station a Marine Corps rapid deployment task force there. To support African operations. We also operate airlift and in-flight refueling elements."

"Will Takigawa come?"

Stein and I have worked with Ken Takigawa before. A Delta Force veteran, he's a capable sniper and weapons specialist. His relaxed, light-hearted manner makes him a welcome partner when everyone is under stress. Upon leaving the service, he started a business training police forces and security professionals. Occasionally worked as a freelance contractor.

"Yes, and Ballard. Will Heth Crockett join you?"

More good news. Ballard is a retired 18-Echo, a communications sergeant. Another Delta veteran we've worked with before.

"Heth will come, but she needs a ride."

"We're flying Takigawa out of Lewis-McChord. They'll pick her up on the way east."

"How quickly can they get here?"

"Sometime Thursday. I'll message you as soon as I have the details."

I turn my head, study Julia's sleeping features. Pale and drawn, but an improvement. Her skin is no longer the color of wet cement.

"What about the girl?" I ask. "Did biometrics turn anything up?"

"Afraid not," Stein says. "We're continuing to search the databases. Running everything twice."

Damn. At least Julia is recovering. It's possible that when she wakes up, she'll tell me something. "What about Orlov?"

"The last time he showed up was September, last year. Ukraine launched attacks on Russian positions east of Kharkov. All the Russians had in that sector was a battalion of militia. The Azov regiment encircled them. Orlov volunteered to lead a rescue force into the cauldron. *Vozdushnodesantnye voyska Rosii.*" Stein pauses. "You speak Russian. Did I say that right?"

"Close enough. *Desantnye* comes from the French *descente*. They're Blue Berets—VDV paratroopers."

"It was considered a suicide mission. They jumped under fire from two hundred feet. With the militia, they broke out and executed a fighting withdrawal. Gave the Russian army time to stabilize the front, broke the back of the Ukrainian offensive. Orlov was awarded the Order of St George Second Class. Russia's highest authority personally hung it around Orlov's neck."

"Isn't he a heroic son of a bitch."

"Two thirds of their casualties were VDV, and most were killed in their parachutes. After that, Orlov disappeared. There was speculation that he was under consideration for greater things. Using a man like that to fight in meat grinders was like having a race horse pull a plow."

"So whatever he's up to right now is more important than saving Russia from a Ukrainian offensive?"

"That," Stein says, "is the implication."

"BREED."

I turn my head to find Julia sitting up on her cot. She's naked, knees pressed together, arms folded over her breasts.

"How are you feeling?"

Dumb question, but we have to start small.

Julia manages a weak smile. "Better. Where are my clothes?"

I point to the floor next to her cot, where I've stacked the tourist T-shirts and makeshift shorts. "Salazar is laundering your other things. They'll be dry tomorrow."

Julia gets up, puts on a T-shirt and a pair of the shorts. Cinches the drawstring of the track pants tight around her hips. Slides her tennis shoes onto her bare feet.

I watch her dress. Somehow, after all we've been through together, it would be silly for me to turn around. She doesn't protest.

The girl sits back down on the cot. Sits very straight, as though she is a guest at a high-end social. "I am sorry, Breed."

"Why?"

"You know why."

Julia's pale features flush and heat rushes to my scalp. She remembers everything.

"Don't worry about it. Nothing happened."

"Alright." The girl's voice is only a little above a whisper, but it is not as hoarse as it was hours ago. We have concluded an agreement. Sealed with a minimum of words. "I'm hungry. Have you anything to eat and drink?"

"Yes. Do you think you can keep it down?"

"I will try."

I open a plastic bag and take out a pair of sandwiches and bottled water. "I'm hungry too," I say. "Do you mind if I eat with you?"

"Of course not."

Julia accepts the sandwich and unwraps it with careful, dainty movements of her long fingers. It's a plain ham and cheese. I hope her ravaged stomach can handle it. She takes a small bite. Chews her food carefully, swallows, and takes a drink of water.

"Don't drink too fast," I tell her. The memory of her violent reaction to slaking her thirst is fresh in my mind.

Julia finishes her sandwich at a measured pace. Drinks half a bottle of water. "I'm still hungry," she says.

I give her another sandwich.

"Julia, who were those men who held you in the car?"

The girl chews thoughtfully. Then she says, "They took me captive in Arles. Kept me locked away in a room, gave me injections with my meals. After a time, I needed the injections more than the meals."

"Where are your parents?"

"I have no parents."

"Where did the men take you prisoner?"

Julia closes her eyes. When she opens them, she meets my gaze and speaks deliberately. "Breed, I am grateful for what you have done. I respect you too much to lie. But I cannot tell you more."

"Fine, we'll take you to the police. They'll find out where you belong."

The girl shakes her head. "No. I cannot go to the police."

She said the same thing the night we took her to the hotel. "Why not?"

"Men are trying to kill me. They have influence. I would not be safe with the police."

Could that be? The Basque is being paid to kill this girl.

They've engaged a gang of killers that stretch from Nice to Cadiz. It's possible they have influence with the police.

Julia frowns. "Last night, I was asleep, but I heard what sounded like shots."

"Men tried to take you."

"Yes. I did not think I was dreaming. Breed, some men want to take me, others want to kill me. I will be honest with you—I need time to think."

"There is not much time. The men who want to kill you are on our trail."

"I know. Breed, I need to rest."

"Alright."

"Now. I could use another of those sandwiches."

17

VALENCIA – TUESDAY, LATE EVENING

The convoy makes camp on a field a quarter of a mile from the town of Cheste. It's a suburb, eighteen miles from the Mediterranean metropolis of Valencia. We've formed our laager, with the two trailers positioned on a diagonal from each other.

Rincón and I stand at the perimeter that faces the town. It's an open field. Behind us, on the other side of the camp, is a vineyard.

I'm pleased. "This is a good security zone. The watchmen have a clear view of anyone approaching."

Last night, we enjoyed a full moon in a clear sky. The rocky terrain around Castillo de Olas was difficult. It offered attackers a lot of cover and concealment. This field is flat as a pancake.

The sky, however, has clouded over. I look up and see high cumuli drifting across the full moon. The clouds begin as a thin veil that first dims the moonlight, then obscures it completely. Minutes later, the clouds pass and the moon shines bright again. Until the breeze draws another curtain across it.

"Did the girl tell you anything?" Rincón asks.

"Nothing we haven't already deduced. She was kidnapped in Arles. Kept prisoner in a room and given heroin injections with her meals. In time she needed the injections more than food. We know the rest."

"Yes." The matador is clearly not satisfied. "What of her family? Her parents?"

"She says she has no parents."

"You believe her?"

"I see no reason to disbelieve her. She was very direct with me. Says she needs time to think."

Rincón scrutinizes me with cynical eyes. "Is that the heroin speaking?"

He's thrown my words back at me. "No. I'm confident she's come through."

"And the police?"

"She says the men trying to kill her have influence with the police. That is not hard to believe."

"Very well, Breed. Sleep well tonight. Tomorrow, I will go to the ring with my *cuadrilla*. You and the girl remain in camp. As soon as the *corrida* is over, we will leave for Seville."

Rincón turns and walks back to his caravan.

The matador sounds like he wants to get rid of us. I don't blame him.

THE SOUND of men shouting startles me awake. I jerk out of bed, rub the sleep from my eyes. Julia's cot is empty.

Damn. I pull on my shoes and run to the gate. It's not completely shut. She must have opened, then closed it, without engaging the latch. She was afraid engaging the latch would have made too much noise.

I jump to the ground. Allegre is running across the field. He's a hundred yards out of the camp. Two hundred yards ahead of him, a flitting ghost. White legs in gray shorts, a light-colored T-shirt, long blond hair.

Men spill out of the caravans. They're confused, trying to figure out what's going on.

Sprinting hard, I catch up to Allegre. "Get back to the camp!"

I pound past him. Julia has reached the first buildings on the edge of the town. She disappears between them.

Son of a bitch. It's well after midnight. We're in an agricultural part of the town. Fields and vineyards. These people are asleep. The buildings are dark.

Where is she? We can't have Rincón's whole team fanning out through the streets, shouting her name. It'll be chaos. And we'll lose the girl.

I move as quickly as I dare, searching left and right. I try to keep quiet, strain my ears to hear running footsteps. Kick myself for being careless. But Julia was through her withdrawal. Weak. She was coherent and intelligent. Running made no sense.

The alleys between the buildings are narrow and surfaced with gravel. Farm tools and equipment rest against the outside walls. I'm a hundred yards into the settlement. Two-story buildings line the path. Buildings constructed in orderly rows and columns.

Voices. Coming from around the corner of a building.

A girl and a man, speaking in low tones.

"*Gyere velem. Elviszlek a régenshez,*" the man says.

What language is that? It's Orlov's voice, but it's not Russian.

"*Nem. Engedj el.*"

Eastern European, but not Russian. Finnish?

Orlov's voice is a hiss. "*Ez a te kötelességed.*"

"*Meg fognak ölni.*" Julia's voice rises in protest.

"*Nem engedem nekik.*"

I step around the corner and show myself. Orlov is my height—he towers over Julia. His posture communicates his intentions. He's trying to convince her to go with him.

They look up when they see me. Julia shrinks with her back to the wall.

"Breed," Orlov says, "this no longer concerns you."

"Like hell. Julia, come with me."

"No." Julia bolts.

I don't think she knows where she's going. All she knows is she doesn't want to be around us.

Orlov and I sprint after her. She turns a corner, runs straight into two men coming the other way. They're dark shapes in the night, carrying guns. One man raises his pistol and points it at us.

Before the man can pull the trigger, Orlov reaches over the girl and grabs the gun. He twists the man's wrist, and the gun discharges into the gravel. Orlov shoves Julia aside and stabs the man in the throat with four pointed fingers. The spear hand penetrates to the man's spine. He lets go of the pistol and chokes.

I grab Julia by the arm, draw the BM from under my shirt. I'll be damned if I'll let go of her again.

Orlov has the first man blocking the second. They're so close the second man can't raise his weapon. Orlov takes the pistol with his left hand, points it at the second man's forehead, and pulls the trigger. There's a sharp crack. The man's eyes open wide—the whites glitter in the powder flare. Black tar bursts from the back of the man's head and he pitches onto his back.

I push Julia behind me.

The first man is still choking. Orlov holds the pistol to the side of the gunman's head and pulls the trigger. The man's head bounces on his neck like a sunflower on its stalk. His knees give way and he crumples.

Three shots pass for backfires. Any more is gunplay.

Slowly, Orlov turns to face us. Holds the pistol, a Beretta 92, at his side.

I point the BM at the Russian colonel. "Orlov, don't."

The colonel stands motionless as Julia and I edge backwards down the alley. I hold my pistol on him with one hand. With the other, I grip Julia's thin arm so tightly my fingers close around the long bone.

Orlov's attention is focused on Julia. When he speaks, he does not sound angry. He sounds like a man counseling a young girl.

"*Ez a te kötelességed.*"

JULIA and I stand opposite each other in the trailer.

"What language was that you were speaking?"

"Hungarian." Julia folds her arms across her chest. Stares at the floor.

"Are you from Hungary?"

"No."

"Where did you learn to speak Hungarian?"

"I speak many languages."

"I bet you do. What did Orlov want?"

"That," Julia says, "is something I can't tell you."

The girl's pissing me off. "How do you know Orlov?"

"I can't tell you that either."

"Okay, why did you run? Did you know he was out there?"

Julia exhales, goes to her cot, and sits down. "No, Breed. I did *not* know he was there."

"Then *why* did you run?"

Hands clasped, elbows on her knees, she stares at me. "Isn't it obvious?"

"I'm a little slow tonight, Julia. Why don't you spell it out."

"Men are trying to *kill* me. Can't you see that so long as I'm with you, they know exactly where I am?"

Damn, she's right.

But there is no way I can let this girl go now. There are too many unanswered questions. She and Orlov know each other. He was trying to persuade her to go with him. He's out there right now. In the dark, with Leandro's men, and those of The Basque. I don't even know who those two men he killed were working for.

It's three o'clock in the morning.

"Lie in bed," I tell her.

"What?"

I pick up my cot, careful not to disturb my gear. "Lie in bed."

Julia stretches out on her cot, and I set mine down right next to hers. I kick off my shoes, get in, and turn my back on her. Sleep with the BM in my right hand. She's lying next to the wall and I'm on the outside.

"Get some sleep," I tell her. "If you get up, I'll feel it. From now on, you're not going anywhere without me."

18

VALENCIA – WEDNESDAY, MORNING

I stand next to Julia's trailer and watch Rincón drive away to the Cheste bullring. The camp has been stripped to the three caravans, a pickup, and Julia's trailer. The trailer stands by itself at the left rear corner of the camp.

Stein picks up on the first ring.

"What's up, Breed?"

"The girl's doing better. She was strong enough to run away last night. I got her back, but not before Orlov got hold of her for a few minutes. They were speaking in *Hungarian*."

"Is she Hungarian?"

"She says no, she speaks many languages. But why would she and Orlov default to Hungarian? If she's not Hungarian, she's from that neck of the woods."

"Right. I'm on it."

"Anything on Takigawa and Heth?"

"Yes. They should arrive at Morón by noon tomorrow."

"Stein—they need to bring weapons."

"What are you looking for?"

"M4s or H&K 416s for Takigawa and Ballard. Three H&K Mark 23s with suppressors, one long-barreled AR-15 with a scope."

"Guns are illegal in Spain."

"Hasn't stopped The Basque and Gypsy King. We can get anything through the gates of Morón if *you* say so."

"Okay. Just don't make me look bad."

Stein signs off. I pocket my phone and go to Rincón's caravan. It's parked next to Julia's trailer.

Inside, Julia has changed into her freshly laundered jeans and T-shirt. She's sitting on the leather sofa, elbows on the table, face in her hands. When she takes them away, her eyes are red and her cheeks are wet. She's been crying.

"What's wrong?" I ask.

Julia sniffles and shakes her head. With a sleeve, she wipes her eyes. "How long will they be?" she asks.

"Bullfights don't start till late afternoon, and they last about two hours. I reckon they'll be back around six o'clock this evening."

"What are we supposed to do till then?"

The door has a window in it. Next to the door is another window, behind one of the sofas. The windows are covered by white cloth curtains on narrow rods. I make myself comfortable on the sofa opposite Julia. Lift a corner of the curtain and peep out.

"You can tell me your story. It'll help me to help you."

Julia stiffens. "Not yet."

I take out the BM and set it on the table.

Julia gives me an encouraging smile. "Why don't you tell me yours?"

"Are you kidding? You tell me nothing and expect me to tell you about me?"

"There's no harm in that."

"How can you be sure?"

"You and Colonel Orlov know each other."

Observant little witch. She's good with words. Knows how to fish for information. "How do you figure that?"

"It was obvious by the way you addressed each other."

"We met a long time ago." I shift the curtain a fraction of an inch. Now I can watch the trailer without lifting the cloth.

"That means you are in the same business," she says.

I say nothing.

"You think he will come again?" Julia asks.

"Don't you?"

Orlov will kill me if he has to. If Julia won't go with him peacefully, he'll take her by force.

"If he doesn't, those other men will. When we get to the next city, let me out. I will disappear."

"Not a chance."

Last night, we crossed another line. Before she emerged from withdrawal, we were caring for her. Now, we are holding her against her will. The whole business is getting more complicated.

"Breed, I'm grateful for what you've done. More than you understand. But you *must* let me go. Those men will kill me."

"I won't let that happen."

Julia buries her face in her hands. "That's what Orlov said."

"Right. He'll bodyguard you all the way back to Russia."

The girl looks at me through bloodshot eyes. "And you? You will protect me all the way to the United States?"

"I'd take a bullet for you. What more do you want?"

"I will not allow the United States to own me. No more than I will allow Russia to own me. *No one* owns me."

The vehemence with which the girl speaks is shocking. I turn my head and stare at her. "Who *are* you?"

Julia shrugs. Stares at the tabletop.

BEFORE THE SUN CAME UP, I moved Julia into Rincón's caravan. I didn't want Orlov, The Basque, and the Gypsy King to know where she was. Now, if any of them make a move, they'll storm the trailer.

The vineyard and the field are deserted. So are the buildings on the other side. It looks like everyone has gone into town for the celebrations. This is Tenebrae—Holy Wednesday. It marks the day Judas plotted with the chief priests to betray Jesus. There will be a service that involves extinguishing candles on a Tenebrae hearse. This will be followed by a procession and the *corrida* at the end of the day.

I take out a length of clothesline.

"Put your hands behind your back and cross your wrists," I say.

"No."

"If I leave the caravan, I can't trust you not to run."

"I promise I won't."

"After last night?" I shake my head. "Not good enough."

I bind Julia's wrists tightly behind her back. Take another length of clothesline and bind her ankles together. Sit her comfortably on the sofa, go back to the curtain.

"You think Orlov's coming?"

"*Someone* is coming."

Hours pass. I change positions regularly, but my position is uncomfortable. I'm having a tougher time of it than Julia, because she's sitting straight on the sofa. I'm twisted around

sideways to look out the window, and my neck is getting
stiff.

"Breed, this is silly."

"Be quiet."

Two black Toyota Hilux pickups are approaching. They
drive fast on the road Rincón used to go into town. These
guys know exactly what they're doing. They stop sixty feet
from the camp, and four men get out.

Right away, I recognize The Basque. Armand Le Cagot
dismounts the second Hilux and stands next to it while his
hitters get ready. Two men from the first Hilux, and the
driver of The Basque's truck. They reach into their vehicles,
haul out Z84 submachine guns and satchels of spare
magazines.

My stomach tightens and I swallow. It's the feeling I get
before combat. Adrenaline courses through my system. I
reach under the table and take two perfume bottles from the
tin bucket. Stuff the BM into my hip pocket and hold one
bottle in each hand.

Timing is everything. The Basque waits at his Hilux
while his men approach the trailer. The three men go to the
back, stand in a row at the foot of the ramp. The trailer gate
is shut, but not locked.

The men on either side look at the man in the middle of
the row. He nods, and they light up the trailer.

The Z84s crackle and the three men dump their mags
into the trailer gate. Riddle it with fully automatic fire. Drop
their empties, reload, and dump another mag each. Reload a
second time.

The trailer gate looks like Swiss cheese. The men run up
the ramp. One man opens the gate. The other two train their

weapons on the interior as it is revealed. The three dash inside.

I open the door of Rincón's caravan and run to the ramp. The three men are inside, staring at an empty trailer.

The perfume bottle is heavy in my right hand. I take a breath, stretch my arm back, and pitch it into the trailer. The men turn in time to see the lump of glass hurtle towards them. Watch me throw myself to the ground.

I don't hear the explosion. The pressure wave boxes my ears and stuns my brain. A blast of hot air rushes over my head. The walls of the trailer vent the explosion out the back. There's an algebraic formula for working out the safe distance at which to detonate explosives. It doesn't work very well with home-made devices. I've probably sustained traumatic brain injury.

Get up, draw the BM. Rush into the trailer, ready to finish off the gunmen.

They're all dead. The inside of the trailer is smoking from the blast. The remains of the men are plastered all over the walls. I mean—*remains*. There isn't enough left of any of the three men to shoot.

I jump from the back of the trailer. Gravel crunches under my shoes and I turn to face the road. The Basque is standing next to his Hilux, trying to figure out what happened.

Shift the second IED to my right hand. The Basque is running around the front of his Hilux. He swings the driver's door open so he can get behind the wheel. I hurl the glass bottle with all my strength. It sails high in the air, passes the top of its arc, and falls short. It plunges onto the hood of the first Hilux and explodes.

There's another concussion. Not as bad as the first,

which occurred in the confined space of the trailer. This blast radiates a spherical shock wave. A quarter of the wave goes straight up. A quarter shatters the windows of the second Hilux and sends The Basque reeling. A quarter of the wave knocks me flat on my ass.

The final quarter goes straight down and turns the driver and engine compartments of the Hilux into a canoe. The Japanese make strong vehicles. I'll give them that. The chassis holds up. I don't think the blast knocked the wheels out of alignment. But the cab and engine compartment are hollowed out and squashed. When the smoke clears, they're empty recesses in a mass of twisted steel. Where's the engine block? It's the most solid, bullet and blast-resistant part of a vehicle. It's been driven into the surface of the road.

Shaking his head to clear it, The Basque struggles to his feet and gets into the pickup. He slams the driver's door and starts it up.

My ears are ringing. Sort of. They're ringing inside my head, but I can't hear any sounds from outside my skull. I draw the BM. Watch The Basque engage the transmission and roll the Hilux.

Is The Basque going to run? No. He floors the gas and sends the Hilux racing straight toward me. I hold the BM in an isosceles and fire at the charging pickup. The blast shattered its windshield, so I'm slinging rounds straight at Le Cagot's head. That big face with the mad eyes, hiding behind a salt-and-pepper beard. He plants his left hand on the wheel at the twelve o'clock and ducks behind the dash.

I throw myself to one side as he roars past. He races twenty yards across the road and spins the wheel. The Hilux rocks on its suspension as The Basque turns around in a spray of gravel. Prone, I extend the BM in an isosceles as he floors the gas a second time and takes another run at me.

All this stuff about stopping a vehicle by firing at its engine block is crap. If you want to stop a car, you *kill the fucking driver*. Survivors of truck bombs at checkpoints in Iraq learned that the hard way. Again, I pound rounds straight through the frame of the shattered windshield. Again, Le Cagot holds the wheel steady with one hand and ducks his head.

The slide of the BM locks back. The Hilux races away toward town.

It was a silent movie. The gunshots, the engine sounds, the screech of tires and brakes—I heard none of it.

I get up, go back to the trailer, and look for the Z84s. They're rugged weapons. As far as I can tell, they are still operational. I sling them across my chest and shoulder so they dangle at my right hip. I locate two of the dead men's satchels of spare magazines and throw them over my left shoulder. The third satchel is gone. Probably in pieces. A number of loaded magazines are scattered among the debris and human remains.

The remains include three slabs of red meat and white bone that look like slaughterhouse carcasses. The most resilient component of the human skeleton is the spinal column. The rest of the bones are readily disarticulated. Meat is easily blown off or vaporized. The spine, with its hard dorsal and ventral wings, typically remains intact.

That's how you count casualties after an artillery strike.

My duffel and the bags of spare clothing are shredded. Now I see why the devastation inside the trailer is so total. The blast from the glass bottle I threw served as a detonator. It set off the solid explosive packed in the plastic bag. The whole lot went up together. I should have taken the stuff with me to Rincón's caravan.

We learn.

I exhale through puffed cheeks, walk down the ramp. The Basque is a blunt instrument. No polish, no class. Drives straight to the target and blazes away. The Gypsy King is crafty. Bolt cutters, knives. A devious son of a bitch.

I stride to Rincón's caravan. There is one good thing—we now have three submachine guns, two pistols, and lots of ammo.

For next time.

19

VALENCIA – WEDNESDAY, EVENING

"**A**re you *crazy*, Breed?"
Julia, Salazar and I sit around the table in
Rincón's caravan. I've untied the girl, and she's
eating another ham and cheese sandwich. The matador
stands over us. Draws back the curtain and looks out the
window at the flattened Hilux. There's a lot of twisted metal,
but it didn't burn. Tendrils of smoke issue from hot grease
and motor oil.

"I'm sorry, Maestro. The trailer will be fine. We'll wash
the pieces out with a hose. I'll pay for a new gate. It'll be as
good as new."

"Oh, yes." Rincón can't conceal the sneer in his voice. "Of
course. Wash the pieces out. Why did I not think of that.
What about the truck, *hombre*? Have you thought about
that?"

I've regained my hearing, but I have a headache. Minor
TBI, but otherwise I'm fine.

"As a matter of fact, I have."

"*Digame.*"

"There's a tributary of the Rio Jucar on the other side of that vineyard. We'll push it into the river."

"Is it deep enough?"

"We'll find out."

Rincón turns to Salazar. "Have there been complaints from the town?"

"Nothing, Maestro. As far as we can tell, everyone was at the *Miércoles Santo* procession. And, of course, the *corrida*."

The matador pulls up an easy chair and folds himself into it. "Breed, you have the luck of a devil. Salazar, you and Breed take care of it. We leave as soon as it's done."

I turn to Julia. "Let's go."

"I would not miss this for the world," Julia says.

"I wasn't giving you a choice."

20

MORÓN – THURSDAY, MORNING

The stone sign proclaims that we are approaching Base Aérea de Móron. During the cold war, this was a Strategic Air Command B-47 base. Since then, it's gone through a number of evolutions. Now it is a Spanish Air Force base. The facility hosts a United States Marine Corps rapid deployment force.

We drove all night to get here. Salazar arranged for the *cuadrilla* and ranch hands to drive in shifts while we slept. Rincón disappeared into his luxury bedroom, not to be seen again until breakfast.

Stein messaged me that we should meet Takigawa, Heth and Ballard at the main gate. To avoid attracting attention, we unhitch the pickup from Julia's trailer and drive the last mile to the base in two Volkswagens. Salazar drives one, Allegre the other. Julia and I ride with Salazar in the front seat of the blue pickup.

The approach to the base is on a long, straight highway. The hot Andalusian terrain is flat. The base has been built on a sizzling skillet. It's early spring. I don't want to know what this place will feel like in summer. The approach is lined with tall palm trees. All the vegetation looks dusty. In the distance, the mountains are a pale blue string of teeth.

I check my watch. It's almost ten o'clock. The main gate is flanked by two guard houses manned by Spanish Air Police. White stone with brown tile roofs. The perimeter is guarded by a fifteen-foot chain-link fence topped with barbed wire. That might stop human intruders, but security takes no chances. Ten feet ahead of the fence is a solid barrier of concrete bollards painted with diagonal black and white stripes. The war on terror has shown time and again that terrorists use vehicles as weapons.

The drive curves in a gentle arc in front of the base. We pull over onto the shoulder thirty feet from the entrance so we don't block the gate.

"Wait here," I say.

It's not a good idea to park across the street from a military installation without identifying yourself. This is an active base for a wing of Eurofighter Typhoons.

I dismount the pickup. Allegre and I walk toward the gate, speak with the Air Police. We are not seeking access. We are meeting American friends at ten o'clock. The Air Police acknowledge, motion for us to wait at the vehicles. One of them speaks into a squad radio Velcroed to his left shoulder.

Allegre and I walk back to the pickups. I take out my phone and message Takigawa.

We're outside.

Takigawa responds within seconds. *On the way.*

I squint in the harsh Andalusian sun. Two men and a girl step through the gate. I wave, and the first man raises his hand in greeting.

Operators are funny. Whenever we dress in casual clothes, we all look alike. It's our off-post uniform. We think we're gray men, going incognito in the field, but we can spot each other a mile away. We have a *look*. We're all fit. Most guys have tats. Then there are the clothes. Usually Oakley desert boots, the kind we wore in Afghanistan and Iraq. Levi's jeans or Kühl tactical pants. Work shirts long enough to conceal a Glock. Appendix carry, of course. Anything from five days' stubble to a full beard. Then—the bent-bill ball cap.

Gator glasses are optional. I usually go with mil-spec shooting glasses.

Yeah. Would never think these are team guys.

Takigawa's half Japanese. Six feet tall, with a barrel chest. He wears a perpetually half-amused expression behind a well-kept beard. A consummate professional, he's quick to laugh and keeps things light. His eyes are shielded by a pair of Ray-Bans. Uniform of the day. He looks left and right, nods to the Air Police, and marches straight toward us.

Ballard's an 18-Echo with a nerdy look. Like yeah, the stereotypical comms guy who grew up building radios in shop class. Six-foot-three and gangly. Wears black plastic birth control glasses. Army issue. The kind you get for pennies at any PX. Despite his harmless appearance, Ballard is competent at every specialty in an OD-A. Like Takigawa and myself, he was selected for Combat Applications Group.

Takigawa and Ballard each carry two olive drab duffel bags on straps over their shoulders. It's not hard to imagine what they contain. Changes of clothes packed around weapons and ammunition.

Heth Crockett's pretty. Five-seven, average build, tight from an active lifestyle. Hard work on a ranch. Riding, hiking and working as a guide for hunting parties. Blond, with a dusky complexion from her half Salish blood. Your rosy-cheeked girl next door. She's wearing Levi's, a T-shirt, and a white ten-gallon hat. A khaki canvas bag is slung over her right shoulder.

The three don't waste time walking toward us. There's a confidence in their step. They know exactly what they're doing, and why they're here. Takigawa and Ballard are on contract to Stein. Heth Crockett has done a handshake deal with me.

We greet each other with hugs and shoulder slaps. Ballard and Takigawa throw their duffels in the cargo bed of Allegre's pickup. Takigawa gets in front with Allegre. Ballard sits on the back seat. Stretches out so he can look through the rear window.

Heth and I get in the back seat of Salazar's truck. He and Julia sit in front. I introduce everyone. We drive back to the convoy and I message Heth.

Stick to her like glue.

Heth's smiley response has gritted teeth.

WHEN WE REJOIN THE CONVOY, Allegre goes to hitch the pickup to Julia's trailer. Salazar leads our little group to Rincón's caravan. The matador steps from the door to greet us.

Rincón, straight and aristocratic as ever, shakes hands with Takigawa and Ballard. When he comes to Heth, he tilts his head with courtesy. He is wearing a black *chaleco* jacket with gold embroidery, and a flat-topped gaucho hat with a wide brim.

"Ah, Ms Crockett. Charmed."

The maestro's manner completely disarms the girl. "Call me Heth. Are you the bullfighter?"

"That is my profession, yes. I think of it as an art."

"I want to see you fight."

"I would be honored if you would come to the *Maestranza* on Sunday."

"I'd love to."

"Salazar will see to it that you all have tickets. The best, at the *barrera*, in the shade."

We go inside the caravan. Rincón hangs his hat on a hook on the wall.

"Maestro, Takigawa and Ballard are here to help," I tell the matador. "We'll be safer if Leandro and The Basque try anything. As soon as we arrange a safe house in Seville, we'll get out of your hair. You've risked enough for us."

"Nonsense," Rincón says. "Your plans are your own, of course. But please... stay at my ranch over Semana Santa. Until the *corrida*."

Heth looks at me with a pleading expression.

"If we won't put you out."

"Not at all."

Rincón turns to Salazar. "It is settled, then. We will arrive at the ranch by noon. You shall have rooms in *La Casa Grande*."

"Your men know we've encountered problems," I say.

"Yes."

"Please spread the word that my friends and I will be carrying weapons. We will not be obtrusive, but I want everyone to understand. They are here to protect us and Julia."

Takigawa and Ballard open their duffels and lay their weapons on the table. Two M4 carbines and one long-barreled AR-15. The AR-15 is equipped with a bipod, Picatinny rail, and a Steiner 3x-15x variable power scope with a first focal plane reticle.

"We didn't know what you'd need," Takigawa says.

"Three to ten times should be plenty." I look at Heth. "Want to zero it for us tomorrow morning?"

"I want to learn about bullfighting."

"Bullfighting is not for everyone," Rincón says. "Perhaps we can test you against some of our calves. Try your hand at a *beccerada*."

"What's that?"

"A bullfight against young bulls."

"I'm in."

"We practice in the afternoon." Rincón's approach is smooth as butter. "That leaves you the morning to calibrate your rifle."

Takigawa sets three Heckler & Koch Mark 23 semiautomatic pistols on the table. A leather bag contains suppressors.

"Will you run suppressed?" Takigawa asks.

"I won't, but you guys should zero *one* of them with a suppressor."

"I'll do mine in the morning."

Most people are not aware that mounting a suppressor affects a pistol's shot placement. The harmonics of a pistol are affected much more than those of a rifle. At distances as short as ten feet, a pistol's sights must be re-aligned when a suppressor is attached.

I take one of the Mark 23s. Do a three-point check and insert a magazine. Chamber a round, decock the weapon, and slide it into my waistband. I take the BM, drop the mag, and rack the slide. Catch the loose round and squeeze it into the magazine. I do a three-point check and hand the weapon to Heth.

"What's *this* for?"

"One of us should be with Julia at all times. If *you* are with her, you need to be armed."

"I've never shot anybody. I didn't come to Spain to kill people."

I hope it doesn't come to that. When I asked Heth to come, all I wanted was a companion for Julia. Heth's ability to shoot is a bonus.

"Of course not. Are you going to let them kill *you*?"

Heth frowns. She's supposed to be on vacation, but this is part of the deal. She does her own check, loads the pistol, and safeties it. Sticks it in her waistband, tugs her T-shirt down.

Julia looks troubled.

Ballard takes one Mark 23 and Takigawa the other. Each takes a canvas satchel of M4 magazines and one carbine. I hand the AR-15 and scope to Heth. "Yours," I say. "Zero it at 3x for a hundred yards. Work out a set of holdovers."

I reach under the table and pick up one of the Z84s that I liberated from The Basque's men. Hand it to Takigawa. "This is what The Basque's men have been using."

"Haven't seen one of these in a long time."

"No. They won't be any good over fifty yards. The Gypsy King's men like to use knives, but I saw one of them with an MP5. It's entirely possible they have more modern weapons."

"The Gypsy King. Where'd you come up with that one?"

"That's what he looks like. Leandro Gabarri. A real piece of work."

I turn to Rincón. "We have three extra submachine guns. Let's train some of your men. At any one time we'll have a security force of seven, not including yourself. Ballard can run a familiarization session tomorrow morning. Takigawa will devise a watch schedule."

"I will see to it."

"You saw what The Basque is capable of. We need to be ready."

"I saw what *you* are capable of."

21

RANCHO RINCÓN – THURSDAY, AFTERNOON

The road from Morón to Seville stretches west over flat country. There are some low rolling hills, but they are so low they barely move the needle. This countryside lies on a vast plain west of the Cordillera mountains. North and west of Seville lie the foothills of the Sierra Morena range.

The convoy drives over a well-maintained highway. Turns off onto a secondary road toward Rancho Rincón. Bulls graze on the fields, herded by vaqueros—Spanish cowboys—on horseback.

"A fighting bull must not see a man on foot until he is brought to the ring," Rincón says. "This is Spanish law. Then, when the bull sees this annoying creature waving a red *muleta*, he will charge without hesitation."

The matador is sitting in the front passenger seat of his Mercedes. Salazar is at the wheel. Heth, Julia and I sit on the wide leather bench in the back. We lead the convoy, stretched over a quarter of a mile of Andalusian highway.

My eyes flick constantly over the cars that pass us, those

parked at roadside stops. I know that Takigawa and Ballard
are doing the same. Ballard is sitting in the blue pickup that
brings up the rear. Takigawa rides in the pickup that tows
the horse trailer.

I would not put it past The Basque to try an attack on the
road.

"There it is," the matador says. "Rancho Rincón. I have
worked all my life for this."

Rincón's ranch rises from the Seville plain on our right.
The Sierra Morena form an azure backdrop to the buildings.
I can make out three from this angle. Two big industrial
barns and a sprawling two-story ranch house.

The Mercedes slows and turns into a paved road. There
is a tall wooden gate that frames the entrance. The crosspiece is adorned with a circular metal logo that consists of
two interlocked *R*s. The *R*s, set in the circle, look like a
brand.

As we approach the ranch, I see there are more buildings. The ranch house, the residential heart of the property,
is set on high ground to the west. The two large barns are set
to the north and east so as to form a U. I assume they contain
stables, bullpens, and hay barns. There is a paved driveway
in the center of the horseshoe, where vehicles can park.

Behind the east barn is a circular fenced area a hundred
yards across. I see it has been equipped with a *barrera*.
Chutes lead from the barn. The chutes open through gates
into the arena. Rancho Rincón has its own bull ring. A third
of the ring's outer wall has been built with white stone. The
remainder is a wooden fence. It looks like the plan is to build
a stone wall all around, but the work has not been
completed.

Two bunkhouses sit next to the barn on the crosspiece of

the U. A water tower peeps above the rooftops. Men and women walk back and forth between the buildings. It looks like there are more structures to the north, but they are obscured by the barn and bunkhouses.

"When I retire," Rincón says, "I will raise my fighting bulls. Already the Rincón breed is gaining a reputation. One day, the breed will be as great as Miura."

"What's a Miura?" Heth asks.

"Miura bulls are the greatest fighting bulls. They are the bravest and the most aggressive. No matador can build a reputation without fighting Miuras."

Salazar parks the Mercedes in front of the ranch house.

"This is *La Casa Grande*," Rincón says. "The Big House. We have much room for you and your friends here."

We dismount and look at the Spanish structure. Two stories, of stone and timber. The hacienda architecture is beautiful. A wide porch stretches the width of the house. The wooden roof of the porch is supported by six stone pillars at the front and thick timbers above.

The pickup towing the horse trailer stops and Takigawa dismounts, carrying his duffel and rifle in plain view. The people at the bunkhouses and barns watch him join us. The blue pickup, driven by Allegre, parks next to the Mercedes. The picador and Ballard climb out.

We watch the remainder of the convoy wind its way to a parking lot that must lie on the north side of the ranch, next to the water tower.

A middle-aged couple stand on the porch. The man wears an apron—he must be the cook.

"Carmen," Rincón says. "Fernando. Come help our guests with their things."

Takigawa, Ballard and myself have no trouble carrying

our own gear. My own duffel was blown to shreds when The Basque and his men attacked in Valencia. I've liberated one of Takigawa's. At a roadside stop, I bought more clothing for myself and Julia.

I shoulder the duffel with Heth's AR-15. I spoke with Rincón and asked him to have Heth and Julia bunk in the same room.

The front door opens to a large foyer. To the left is a spacious living room with comfortable furniture and a big fireplace. A wooden carving of a bull stands in a hall between the living room and the rest of the ground floor. The interior of the Big House is cool. Discreetly placed on the floor and ceiling are vents for central air conditioning.

"To the right is the library," Rincón says. "At the end of the hall is the dining room and the kitchen. The kitchen opens to the back."

"We do not use the kitchen much in the Big House," Fernando says. "There is a cookhouse outside. I do my cooking there."

The walls of the living room are decorated with the heads of bulls. I assume they are Rincón bulls, slain in bull-fights. These are bulls that turned in exceptional performances.

A grand staircase with a polished mahogany banister extends from the foyer to the second floor. Carmen leads the way and shows us to our rooms.

Heth and Julia share a room at the top of the stairs. It is on the east side of the house, where it will catch the morning sun. It overlooks the driveway. Ballard and Takigawa share the room next to the girls. I occupy one across from theirs.

At the end of the second-floor hall is Rincón's master bedroom. I assume it is the largest in the house, and occupies the entire western half of the second floor. It will have the best view of the mountains.

My phone buzzes. It's Stein: *Call me.*

I motion to Julia and Heth to precede me down the stairs. Rincón stands in the living room, shoulders back, hands on his hips.

"He's so cool," Heth whispers.

Rincón invites everyone to sit with him in the living room and asks Fernando to serve us drinks. I hold my phone up to indicate I have to make a call. Excuse myself and go back outside.

I WALK AROUND to the shady side of the house and sit with my back to the wall. The sun hasn't set, and the heat is stifling. I'm ready to walk to Guyana for a Kool-Aid. I hit Stein's speed dial.

"Breed, the Hungarian that Julia was speaking with Orlov did the trick. You don't know what you have."

"Tell me."

"Julia is Princess Gyula of Marethia."

My brain connects the dots instantly. I remember the news story that streamed on Palm Sunday. I watched it while waiting for the bullfight in Rodilhan.

"Marethia is a small principality in the Carpathians. It sits on a quad-border between Hungary, Ukraine and Romania. It controls the Palvet Pass. It's the only route through the Carpathians through which weapons can flow year-round from Romania to Ukraine."

"I saw a story on the news."

"Yes. The prince was scrupulously neutral in his relations with Europe, Ukraine and Russia. Marethia is a

wealthy country, with a rich financial industry. It thrives on
its independence from EU regulations. The prince refused to
let weapons shipments pass between Romania and Ukraine.
Two weeks ago, there was a coup. Unknown assailants
entered the royal residence and rounded up the prince and
his family. Herded them into the courtyard and shot them."

"Was the prince so unpopular?"

"No, quite the opposite. By all accounts, the prince and
the royal family are loved. The regent, who was supposed to
take over, fled to Budapest. The prime minister seized power.
As often happens, a small but committed group can dominate a disorganized population."

"The killers missed the regent. And they missed Princess
Julia."

"Gyula. Yes, she also goes by Julia. She was away at
school in Geneva. Boarded with an elderly couple. The
elderly couple were found murdered. The girl living with
them couldn't be found. They kept to themselves. No one
had details on their boarder. The Swiss police didn't know
who they had either."

"Wasn't she missed from school?"

"It's Easter break. The school's closed and students have
scattered over a dozen countries. To top it off, the new
government claims the entire royal family was murdered.
The whole world assumed Julia was with them."

"Somehow, she ended up in Arles. How did Orlov get
involved?"

"After his heroics in Kharkov, he was given a diplomatic
assignment. He was an attaché at the Russian embassy in
Marethia. You see, NATO wanted the prince to allow them to
use the Palvet Pass to move weapons. They held out EU
membership and NATO protection if he agreed."

"Of course, the prince told them to fuck themselves. EU membership would kill his country's finance industry."

"He didn't use those words. Well, maybe in Hungarian. Marethia was once part of the Austro-Hungarian empire. They still enjoy close relations with Hungary. Orlov is a walking death machine. But he can be very charming and diplomatic. Marethia's neutrality is important to Russia. They sent Orlov to liaise with the royal family and keep the prince sweet."

"That's how Julia and Orlov know each other."

"They met at court, when Julia visited at Christmas. Julia speaks Russian. Orlov speaks Hungarian. When the prince and his family were murdered, everything changed. The prime minister wants to join the EU, join NATO, and permit passage of weapons through the Palvet Pass."

"None of that is good for Russia. How did they find out Julia was alive?"

"Orlov built a relationship with the royals. The youngest children called him Uncle Max. He knew Julia was in Geneva. When the prime minister announced the entire family was dead, Orlov knew it was a lie. He reported to Moscow—the killers missed one daughter. The order came from Russia's highest authority. Orlov is to fetch Princess Julia and convey her to the regent."

"How did he track her to Arles?"

"She made it easy for anybody who was looking for her —she used a credit card to buy her train ticket."

"Guess they didn't teach her tradecraft in school."

"It's also likely they had her phone number. Russia has the technology to geolocate mobile phones. Marethia might not have that technology, but the prime minister is backed by security services that do."

"Any idea which ones?"

"Yes, but I'm not saying. Except—it isn't us."

"How comforting."

"We can't control *every* ally who gets desperate. It's safe to say the prime minister of Marethia hired men to kill the royal family. Tracked the princess to Arles, and hired The Basque to finish her off. Somehow, in Arles, she ran into the Gypsy King." Stein takes a breath. "Princess Gyula is now under the protection of US contract operators. We're in talks with the State Department about what to do with her."

"Sounds like an easy decision to me."

"The State Department is going crazy. This incident could fracture our alliances. What we do with Princess Julia is well above my pay grade."

"Does she have a choice?"

"Between the Gypsy King, The Basque, and Orlov? Right now, she's with the good guys."

Julia's words echo in my mind. *No one owns me.*

I'm not sure we'll have the last word. Russia's *highest authority* instructed Colonel Maxim Orlov to *fetch* the Princess Julia.

And kill anybody who gets in the way.

I WALK BACK inside the Big House. Find Rincón entertaining the group in his living room. It's beautifully finished, with paneled walls and rich mahogany furniture. Collections of bullfighting swords are mounted on the walls with photographs of the maestro. They show him in bullrings all over the world.

Heth leans forward, elbows on her knees, listening to the maestro with rapt attention. Takigawa and Ballard are relaxed, sipping beers. For them, this is about guys chilling around a campfire, sharing stories.

Legs crossed, Julia sits demurely in a corner of the sofa. She's polite, but not particularly interested.

I greet everyone, then gesture to Julia. "Can we speak?"

"Of course."

Julia rises from the couch and I lead her into the library. Four pairs of eyes follow us out of the room.

The library is huge, with shelves that rise to the ceiling. There are two wooden stepladders on wheels. They slide on brass rails mounted above the shelves. There's another leather living room set in the middle of the room. It's flanked by two large reading tables with green-shaded lamps. Paintings of flamenco dancers, matadors and fighting bulls adorn the spaces between bookshelves.

I lower myself into an easy chair and stretch my legs. Motion for Julia to make herself comfortable on the sofa. I luxuriate in the cool air. Julia looks tired. She has not yet recovered from her ordeal. Indeed, she only came through the worst of her withdrawal a couple of days ago.

"Alright, Breed." Julia folds her hands on her lap. "Here I am."

"I thought we should properly introduce ourselves, princess."

Julia smiles sadly. "You know."

"I know some things. Not everything."

"It must have been my conversation with Colonel Orlov. In Hungarian."

"That helped narrow down the investigation."

"What do you want, Breed?"

"I want you to tell me everything."

She does.

22

RANCHO RINCÓN – THURSDAY, EVENING

The *Institut Pour la Culture des Jeunes* occupied an elegant villa that overlooked Lake Geneva. There, two hundred and fifty young girls obtained an International Baccalaureate. Their placement rate at the best colleges and universities was one hundred percent. Alumni continued to Harvard, Yale, Princeton, Oxford and Cambridge. They were the daughters of prime ministers, kings, queens, and oligarchs of all stripes.

Princess Gyula of Marethia, known to her friends as Julia, was a good student. Not the best, not the worst. She sat comfortably in the middle of the class. Her father had taught her that to get on in life, it was often best to be in the middle. The girl no one noticed. Because her station would ensure that she would always draw more attention than anyone could want.

She studied English, French, German, and Latin. She read Dostoyevsky in Russian. No one at the school spoke her native Hungarian. She studied algebra and physics. She studied world history and civics.

But—the *Institut Pour la Culture des Jeunes* taught its students more. Princess Julia learned how to slice an orange with a knife and fork. She learned to section it with the skill of a surgeon. She spread the peel like the petals of a flower. When she was done, a perfect orange sat in the middle of the arrangement.

All the while she sliced and peeled the orange, she was expected to maintain perfect posture and converse about the issues of the day. She had to be articulate, charming, and diplomatic. Cope with difficult personalities. Deflect controversial topics.

Julia was enjoying spring in Geneva. The *Institut's* Easter break was two weeks long, plus weekends. The *Institut* always released its students well in advance of Easter because international students had to travel. Julia sat at a café by the lake, watching the Jet d'Eau fountain launch thousands of gallons skyward. She wondered mischievously what it would be like to empty a box of laundry detergent into the water.

Her attention was focused on the lake. This was where water from Lake Geneva entered the Rhône and began its journey to Arles and the Camargue. She paid scant attention to the news that played on the café widescreen.

The word *Marethia* caught her attention. It was her country. She twisted in her seat for a better view.

The Prince of Marethia and the entire royal family have been murdered.

Julia's stomach clenched. Her father, her mother, her brothers and sisters?

*Unknown assailants shot the family in the courtyard of
their home. The Regent has disappeared. Reports suggest
he fled to Hungary.*

It couldn't be. She stared at the screen, fists held to her
mouth. The video showed bodies stretched on cobblestones.
The faces were discreetly blurred, but she could recognize
her mother's shoes and her father's trousers. Blood ran in the
cracks between the stones.

Julia staggered to her feet. The world was spinning and
she thought she would faint. She wanted to call someone,
but there was no one to call. She had to do something, and
all she could think to do was go home.

Lightheaded, she walked to the lakeshore road—the
Quai Gustave-Ador. It felt like her legs belonged to someone
else. She couldn't feel the pavement under her feet. Feared
she would stumble and fall. She flagged a passing taxi and
gave the driver the address of her boardinghouse.

The house was a wooden two-story home in *Eaux-Vives.*
The place wasn't as trendy or fashionable as modern apartments in Moilebeau. The neighbors were elderly and established. The home was walking distance from the lake, but
she wasn't thinking. She paid the driver, got out of the car,
and ran to the front door.

Julia let herself in. The Escoffiers were usually home in the
early afternoon. Their children had grown up, and now worked
at lucrative professions in Zurich. The elderly couple, now in
their sixties, kept their house and rented out spare rooms to
help with expenses. At the moment, Julia was the only boarder.

Her bedroom was on the second floor, across the hall
from the Escoffiers' bedroom. She climbed to the landing

and looked into the bedroom that Monsieur Escoffier had converted to a den. She usually came home to find him working at his computer or reading a book.

Escoffier sat at his desk with his back to her. The computer's screen saver showed a wide, elliptical pattern—a ring viewed from an angle—rotating and changing color against a black background. His hair had gone silver-gray and he had a bald spot in the back.

He's fallen asleep, she thought. Put her hand on his shoulder and shook him. "Monsieur."

When Escoffier didn't respond, she turned him around and gasped. His throat had been torn out. There was a wide gash that extended from one side to the other, and the front of his shirt was brown with blood. His eyes were wide and staring.

Stifling a scream, Julia stepped back into the hall. She rushed to the Escoffiers' bedroom. Madame Escoffier lay on the couple's king-size bed, staring at the ceiling with sightless eyes. There was a round black hole in her forehead. The pillow next to her had a hole in the middle, and a fan of black scorch marks from a muzzle flash.

Julia's stomach rose into her throat. She was about to vomit when a man stepped from her bedroom. He had a gun in his hand. An ugly black pistol pointed at her chest. There was another man behind him, similarly armed.

The man was bald and heavy-set. He wore a black leather jacket and stared at her with a hard gaze. He gestured with his gun. He wanted her to step to one side. Why?

She realized she was standing between the man and the Escoffiers' bedroom window. The man was afraid that if he shot her, the bullet would pass through her body, shatter the window, and alert passersby.

He was going to shoot her as soon as she stepped away from the window.

Julia took half a step. The man raised the pistol and took aim. Faint, Julia raised her hand to the door to support herself. She was still standing in front of the window. Then, with the strength of desperation, she slammed the door in the man's face. The door struck the pistol and knocked the weapon from his hand. Julia turned the lock.

The man swore as he scrambled to pick up his pistol. Julia ran for the window. It was big, the kind that slid open. She got both hands on the frame. Opened it as wide as she could and looked out onto the backyard. The lawn was fifteen feet below her.

The men threw their shoulders against the door. Julia planted one foot on Madame Escoffier's dresser stool and climbed out the window. She grasped the windowsill with her fingers. The rails of the metal frame bit as she allowed her arms and fingers to take her weight. There was a crack. The men had given up trying to break in with their shoulders. They had turned the pistol on the lock.

Julia dangled from the windowsill. She looked down and jumped.

She landed with her feet together. The impact caused her to bend her knees and she fell like a stumbling drunk. Landed on all fours. She was surprised to find herself unhurt.

The men stared down at her.

Julia got to her feet and ran. She ran for the front of the house, for that was where she might find help. She ran, arms and legs pumping with the strength of desperation. She looked back. The men were not following her. They were too big or too scared to jump. They were pounding down the stairs. She was more than two hundred yards away when they burst from the front door.

She could walk to the lake in fifteen minutes. Running, she could get there in five. But the men must have come in a car. If they got in a car, they would overhaul her, and the game would be up.

Julia ran between the buildings and houses. Ran a zigzag route to throw the men off. Her heart pounded, her head seemed ready to burst from fear. When Julia reached the *Quai* she looked left and right. She had no idea what the killers' car looked like. Sweating, she flagged a taxi, dove inside, and told the driver to take her to the train station.

23

RANCHO RINCÓN – THURSDAY, EVENING

J ulia, normally pale, has gone white as a sheet. The memory of the murders in the Escoffier house has shaken her.

"You did well," I say.

"Did I? I ran like a frightened child."

She *was* a frightened child, but I don't tell her that. Not one adult in a thousand would have left that house alive. "Did they follow you to the train station?"

"I don't know. When I got to the train station, I didn't see anyone. But I was afraid they were there. I was afraid there would be *different* men waiting and watching. I bought a ticket on the first train out of Geneva and it took me to Arles."

"How did you meet Leandro?"

Julia takes a deep breath and spreads her hands flat on her knees. "*That* is another story."

· · ·

THE TRAIN STATION in Arles was packed when Julia got off the train. She was alone. She had nothing but her purse and the clothes on her back. She had no idea where to go. She took her phone from her purse. The battery was low, so she went to a convenience shop in the station and bought a universal charger. Bought herself a coffee, plugged in the phone, and used her browser to research Arles.

Julia had to find a place to stay for a while. If she could gather her thoughts, she could think what to do next. Tibor Szabo, the regent, had fled to Hungary. Whoever murdered her family had tried to kill her. Surely they would try to kill him too. Her father trusted Tibor. She had known him all her life. If he was still alive, she had to find a way to contact him.

She wanted to check into a hotel in Arles. But she had left her passport in Geneva. She needed to find a place that did not require identification.

There was another reason not to stay at a hotel. Julia couldn't trust the police. Killers murdered her family to seize power. If the governments of the world recognized the new government, their police forces might cooperate. The French police might share her location with the killers.

Julia decided to go to the tourist heart of Arles and find a bed and breakfast. An inexpensive place to stay that wasn't too fussy about rules and regulations. She got up, packed her phone and charger into her purse, and went in search of transportation.

The queues for taxis and buses stretched around the block. Worse, they didn't seem to be moving. She went to the back of the line and called up the map function on her phone. Tried to figure out how long it would take to walk.

"This is ridiculous," the boy behind her said.

"Yes, it is." Julia studied him. The boy had short brown hair, looked eighteen. He wore a striped rugby shirt and jeans. Carried a blue airline bag over his right shoulder.

"We could be here for hours," he said. "Where are you going?"

"I'm trying to find a bed and breakfast in town."

"Where?"

"Someplace in the city center. I won't be in town long."

The boy looked thoughtful. "There are many such places near the tourism office on Boulevard Clemenceau."

"Where's that?" Julia tilted her phone to show him a map.

"Right here." The boy swiped with his fingers to zoom in on a location close to the Roman Amphitheater. The spot was labeled *Offices de Tourisme de France*.

"I see. Perhaps I will find a place there."

"I am fed up with this queue. I am going to take a minicab. The tourist office is on my way, I can drop you there."

Julia hesitated. She was anxious to leave the station. Her instinct told her it was no good to stay too long in one place. She did not know if the killers had followed her to the station in Geneva. She suspected they might be able to trace her movements. Julia was not naïve. She was aware that credit card usage could be tracked, but she had no choice. She had no other money. She had turned off her mobile phone's tracking function. Still, she thought it might be possible to geolocate the device. The technology was beyond her understanding.

"Alright," she said. "Where are you going to find a minicab?"

"There are always some behind the station," the boy said.

"They are not licensed, so the taxi drivers hate them. What is your name?"

"Julia. And you?"

"I am Jean Claude. Very nice to meet you."

Jean Claude walked across the garage. The pavement was stained with grease from taxis and buses lined up with motors idling. The air was thick with clouds of exhaust fumes. Julia was relieved when they emerged onto the street.

Behind the station was a parking lot. There were rows of parking spaces, almost all of them occupied. Most of the cars were empty. A few had drivers sitting behind the wheel, smoking or reading newspapers.

Jean Claude stepped to the first car with a driver. Spoke to him in French. Julia spoke fluent French. It was clear Jean Claude was negotiating. The driver, a swarthy young man, was firm on his price. Jean Claude agreed, on condition the driver took them to two addresses. First, the tourist information center on Boulevard Clemenceau, then Jean Claude's own destination.

They got into the car together. It was a blue Renault four-door sedan. Jean Claude set his airline bag between them on the bench seat. The interior smelled of cigarette smoke. Julia wrinkled her nose.

"What are you doing in Arles?" Julia asked.

"I am visiting my parents for the Easter holiday. Why are you here?"

"I want to see a bit of the country over Easter."

Julia waited for Jean Claude to ask about her luggage. She had a lie prepared—it had been stolen. The boy did not press her.

The narrow streets were packed with traffic. There were no tall buildings. All were two or three stories. The people on the streets did not look like tourists. In fact, Julia did not think they were getting any closer to the city center.

Jean Claude seemed comfortable. He wasn't inclined to make small talk, and the silence suited Julia.

The driver turned sharply into a narrow alley. At first, Julia thought he was trying to get around a traffic jam. Then she was struck by the absence of people in the alley. Traffic was flowing through the streets at either end.

Several doors were set in the brick walls that lined the alley. The driver stopped the car, and Julia found herself staring at an ugly panel of black wood. The door's paint was cracked and peeling like makeup on a wrinkled old lady.

The door swung inward. A large man with long dark hair and a drooping mustache stepped out. He was wearing black trousers and a brown leather jacket. Before Julia could react, the man jerked her car door open. He reached in, grabbed her by the arm, and dragged her from the car.

Julia screamed and kicked. The man balled his fist and punched her in the belly. The air went out of her with a violent belch. Pain stabbed through her chest and her legs gave way. She wanted to scream from the pain, but could not catch her breath. Lying on the floor, she saw Jean Claude sitting in the car, looking at her. Then the mustached man slammed the door.

Leandro stared at her.

THE GROUND FLOOR of the building was dark and cramped. Julia lay in a narrow hall. On the left was a steep staircase with a wooden banister. Straight ahead was a cramped living room with a sofa and a flat-screen TV. Beyond the living room was a dining alcove and a small kitchen. The place was a hovel.

Leandro jerked Julia to her feet and marched her up the stairs. On the landing, they found themselves in another narrow hall. There were two bedrooms—one to the left, one to the right. Straight ahead was a tiny bathroom. The hall stank of mold.

The bedroom to the left was empty. It had a small window that overlooked the alley. Leandro pushed her into the windowless bedroom to the right. There was a single metal-frame bed with white sheets and pillows with striped pillowcases. The room was lit by a small table lamp with a dim, low-wattage bulb.

Leandro took her purse. Julia clung to its shoulder strap. The gypsy cocked his fist and made to strike her. She let go.

"Give me your watch," he said.

Julia hesitated.

"Do you want me to beat you?"

She gave him the watch.

The fight gone out of her, Julia allowed Leandro to handcuff her to the bed. He produced shiny nickel-plated manacles from his hip pocket. Snapped one cuff around her right wrist and the other around an iron bedpost. She noticed that the bedposts were painted green. The paint had been scraped from the post she was fastened to. Underneath, the post was the color of a lead pipe. The metal itself was scratched.

Julia realized this was not the first time someone had been handcuffed to the bed.

Leandro went out. He took her purse and watch with him. A few minutes later, he returned with a ceramic cocktail tray. The tray had a cork surface. He set it on the table next to the bed. On the cork were a bottle of alcohol, cotton swabs, and a syringe. He straightened her left arm, then swabbed the inside of her elbow. The alcohol felt cold and wet.

"Close your eyes," the gypsy said. "This will calm you. Everything will be fine."

Julia did as she was told. Felt a prick as the needle entered her arm.

Leandro reached under the bed and slid out a blue plastic basin, eighteen inches across. He left it on the floor by the foot of the bed. "This is your toilet," he told her. Then he left the room and took the syringe with him. Julia sat on the bed. Her mind and body were flooded with warmth. It was a wonderful feeling—the outside world went away and she felt at peace. Feet on the floor, Julia slumped sideways and laid her head on the pillows.

WHEN SHE AWOKE, Julia tried to think. She heard voices coming from the room across the hall. Men were speaking Spanish. She understood some of what they were saying, but could not make sense of it. They talked about "the girl." They spoke about Palm Sunday.

Palm Sunday held a special significance for these men. Were they the men who had killed the Escoffiers? If so, why had they not killed her?

The door opened, and Leandro came in with a tray of food and another syringe. He watched her eat and drink. Then he gave her another injection. She sank into a blissful stupor. He picked up the blue basin, full of her urine, and handed it to a man outside the door. Then he took the tray of food and the syringe away.

Julia understood why she had been kept in the window-less room. The dim lamp by her bed was kept on all the time. Without any sense of night or day, without her watch, she lost track of time.

The only sense Julia had of the passage of time was related to her bodily functions. Somehow, Leandro brought the needle whenever she began to feel a need for the medicine. She wondered how he knew. Whenever he brought the needle, he brought food and drink.

She regularly relieved herself. Unable to hold it in, she accepted the indignity of removing her jeans and squatting over the plastic basin. One of the men would take the basin away and rinse it out. She would hear the toilet flush. Occasionally, she would be made to strip. She was pushed down the hall to the toilet and told to shower.

Then Leandro brought her food, but not the needle.

"Will you give me medicine?" Julia asked.

Leandro handed her the tray of food. "Eat," he said.

Julia found her hands shaking as she tried to lift a forkful of paella to her mouth. She managed to swallow two mouth-fuls before handing the plate back to him. "I'm not hungry," she said.

Leandro took the food away and closed the door. Julia lay on her back. The chills overcame her and she shivered for what seemed like hours.

When the gypsy returned, he was carrying the syringe. Julia sat up. She could not look away from the syringe. She needed the medicine. Stretched her arm out, palm upraised. There were needle marks and bruises inside her elbow.

Leandro drew a chair to her bed and sat down. Set the needle on the table next to the lamp. Julia's eyes followed him. "Give it to me," she said. "Please."

The man held up two fingers of his right hand. Touched her cheek and made her look at him. Then he traced his fingertips across her lips. "Kiss them," he said.

Julia recoiled. Her eyes darted with confusion.

"Kiss them," Leandro said.

She felt sick. Leaned forward and gave his fingers a peck.

"You can do better than that." Leandro's voice was chiding. Like a man speaking to a child. Or a dog. He held his fingers out. "Suck them."

"No."

Leandro got up, took the syringe, and walked to the door.

"Please," Julia said. "I'm sick."

Leandro walked out.

JULIA STARES at me across the library. She speaks in a quiet voice. Paints the picture as only an educated, articulate girl can.

"I don't need to know this," I say.

"Don't you see, Breed?" Julia asks. "You're the only one I can tell. I will never speak of these things again."

Lightheaded, I listen to Julia's story.

WHEN LEANDRO RETURNED, Julia sucked his fingers.

"Better than that."

Her mind was focused on the needle that lay on the table. She feigned enthusiasm.

Leandro withdrew his fingers from her mouth and slapped her. "I said, *better than that*. Or I shall leave."

Julia tried harder. Forced herself to focus on the task at hand. Leandro withdrew his fingers and held up his palm.

"Now," he said, "lick it."

IT WAS NOT long before Julia did things she never imagined a girl could do. To satisfy her need for the needle, she debased herself. When she satisfied Leandro, he gave her the needle. When she refused some particularly disgusting demand, he withheld it. He only needed to keep the needle from her long enough. When he returned, she would crawl to him naked and do whatever he asked. She invented new variations to surprise him.

Before long, Julia's world dissolved into the room, Leandro, and the needle. There was nothing else.

Time passed. It had no meaning.

She heard Leandro speaking with the men in the next room.

"Where was he found?"

"In the garbage behind the train station."

"Jean Claude."

"They removed his skin."

"A deboning knife was found next to the carcass."

"Palm Sunday."

"Delivery."

"Did he tell?"

"*¡Pendejo!* Of course he did."

Leandro came into the room and removed the handcuffs. Pushed her to the toilet and made her shower. When she was clean, he made her dress. She pulled on her T-shirt, jeans and shoes. Then he handcuffed her hands behind her back and blindfolded her.

He helped her down the stairs. When she moved too

slowly, he picked her up and carried her down. She heard
the door open and she was pushed into a vehicle. Not the
sedan she had arrived in. This one was bigger. Leandro got
in next to her and another man sat on her other side.

The car drove off.

Julia was swooning in her heroin-induced haze. She
struggled to comprehend what was going on. She wanted to
draw conclusions from what she heard, engrave them on her
brain. When she awakened, she hoped she would not be so
overcome by her need for the drug that she forgot
everything.

Someone had killed Jean Claude, the charming boy who
had betrayed her. Leandro was afraid he had told the killer
where to find her.

Leandro was not with the men who had murdered her
family. If he had been, she would be dead. Kidnapping and
enslaving her was something else. The men who killed her
family and the Escoffiers were still after her.

They drove her to another place. Parked the vehicle in a
garage and left her alone, bound in the car. After a long time,
she began to panic. She felt the need for the drug. Leandro
gave her another shot. The men piled into the vehicle,
started the engine, and drove.

After half an hour, they pulled over onto the side of the
road. Leandro freed her hands and removed her blindfold.
She blinked. It was the first time since she had been
captured that she was allowed to see the outside world.

There was not much to see. Night had fallen. Cars drove
back and forth on the road. Their headlights cut bright
swathes through the darkness. She was in an SUV with four
men. In the front were the driver and a big gypsy who wore
his hair in a man-bun. Leandro sat on her right, another

man on her left. The man on her left was carrying a short submachine gun. He held it low, so it would not be visible from outside the car.

Leandro was happy to release her hands because the heroin had made her docile. They drove further along the road. She saw a big green-and-white sign on the shoulder that said, *Rodilhan*.

The men drove through the town and turned into the parking lot of a low restaurant-bar. The sign in front read *Le Petit Lapin*. The driver parked the car at a slight angle. He occupied two parking spaces. The men sat and waited.

An hour passed, and the gypsies grew nervous. The sounds of accordion music drifted from inside the bar. Julia saw a man step from the bar and stand on the porch. It was Breed.

From a darkened building next door, four men strode purposefully to Leandro's SUV. One of the men was big and muscular, with a full beard. The four men lined up in front of the SUV, drew weapons from under their coats, and started shooting.

"Now," Julia says, "you know everything."

"They're going to try again."

"I'm sure they are. Has our prime minister consolidated his government?"

The young girl seems to have aged ten years. Her expression is grave.

"I don't know. My friends in the United States may have more information soon."

"Dr Tibor Szabo."

"Who's he?"

"The regent. My father's lifelong friend. If anything happened to my father, Tibor Szabo was to lead the government until a proper succession could be arranged."

"I heard on the news that he fled to Hungary."

"Yes, but the same people who murdered my family will try to murder him. I have to speak to him. Together, he and I can fashion a way forward."

I'll raise the question next time I speak with Stein. Her discussions with the State Department must be taking the regent into account.

"Fair enough," I say. "I'll see what I can find out. Now, we should introduce you to the others."

"Not everyone."

"No. Only the folks in the next room need to know. Rincón is our host. My friends are your protection team."

Julia rises to her feet. "Thank you, Breed."

I usher the princess back to the living room.

24

RANCHO RINCÓN – FRIDAY, MORNING

Takigawa has drawn a bull's-eye target on a piece of paper.

We walk from the Big House and cross the driveway. Skirt the barn on the east side. We've since learned that the building contains bullpens, calving pens, and a large hay barn. The bullring lies behind the bullpens. It's a clear area where we can shoot without endangering people. Takigawa pins the target on a post and paces off ten yards. Most close quarters kills are made at a fraction of that distance. He opens a small carrying bag and sets it on the ground. It contains a suppressor, several magazines of .45 ACP ammunition, and a small plastic box of screwdrivers. He draws his Mark 23.

I take my Mark 23 and heft it. When Takigawa has finished, I'll fire a test group of my own. I don't like going into a fight with a weapon I haven't tested.

"Okay," Takigawa says, "to start, I'm going to fire two groups of five. First group unsuppressed, second group suppressed. Let's see how much impact shift we get."

A number of ranch hands gather to watch. I wave them off, make sure they stand behind us.

Takigawa takes a solid firing stance. Two-handed isosceles. His forearms bunch and his blue tattoos ripple. He raises the Mark 23 and fires five rounds. All drill the target in the bull's-eye.

"Tight group," I say. "Pretty good for a weapon right out of the box."

"The armorer worked with it." Takigawa reaches for the suppressor and screws the long tube onto the threaded barrel of the Mark 23. "I do my own checks."

It's axiomatic. *Your* gun is *your* responsibility. I've always been adamant about zeroing and cleaning my own rifle to my schedule. In regular army units, sergeants make troopers clean their weapons regularly. In Combat Applications Group, we know that a rifle requires an optimal amount of fouling to shoot true. A rifle can be *too* clean. It has to be broken in.

"This is a pretty light can," Takigawa says. He assumes his stance a second time, fires another five rounds.

This time the shots make no sound. The .45 ACP rounds are subsonic. That eliminates the supersonic crack of bullets breaking the sound barrier. The suppressor baffles mute the sound of gas exploding from the muzzle. The only sound is the metallic clack of the slide reciprocating. The Mark 23 provides a facility to lock the slide, turning the weapon into a totally silent single-shot killer.

Takigawa and I walk together to the target. The second group remains tight, with only a slight increase in dispersion. The center of the group, however, is two inches lower on the post.

"Will you zero it?" I ask.

"It's fine," Takigawa says. "I know the drop."

That's one of the issues with a suppressed firearm. Will its primary use be suppressed or unsuppressed? If it's going to be a dedicated suppressed weapon, it's worth adjusting the zero. If it's going to be used unsuppressed most of the time, it's enough to know the drop. Takigawa is happy knowing how much to adjust.

I take my pistol and fire a five-round group. Once again, the Mark 23 pounds the rounds right into the bull's-eye. I fire a second group with the same results.

"Can we take a turn?"

Ballard has arrived with Alvaro, Curro, and Allegre. He is carrying a heavy duffel.

"We're done," I tell him. "Have fun."

Ballard opens the duffel and passes the Z84s to the three men. Rincón has chosen them to handle the submachine guns. When Ballard is finished with them, they'll know the basics of weapons safety. They'll be able to shoot and reload. They might even be able to hit something.

"How long will you be?" I ask.

"Couple hours."

"When you're done, ask Rincón to pick six more men. I want us able to rotate shifts. Then swap with Heth. Stay with Julia while Heth zeroes her rifle."

Ballard grins. "I never bodyguarded a princess before."

"First time for everything."

Takigawa and I walk the perimeter. "What do you think?" I ask him.

"It's a tough place to cover." We pass the barn that houses the bull and calf pens. The other barn, on the crossbar of the

U, houses the stables and cow milking pens. Like the bullpens, this barn is huge. It shelters the horses of the picadors, ranch hands, and herdsmen.

Turning the corner, we see the other buildings on the crossbar—the ranch hands' bunkhouse and the *cuadrilla's* bunkhouse. To the right of the *cuadrilla's* quarters, at the end of a drive that circles the ranch, is a large garage. It's not your regular suburban two-car garage. It's as big as a small airplane hangar. It has room for the caravans, the trailers, the SUVs, the Mercedes, and other ranch vehicles.

Between the *cuadrilla's* house and the Big House, we see a corner of Fernando's cookhouse.

"It's as big as a small town," I say. "Must be fifty people living here. There's space for more, depending on the season."

"The terrain isn't as flat as it looks. The ground from the highway is flat, but there are foothills to the west and north. See that tree line?"

I look north to a long line of dusty olive trees that stretches across the field in an east-west direction. "Yes, there's a stream behind it."

Takigawa nods. "You're going to build a ranch next to a stream, aren't you? Rincón draws electricity from the power lines that run along the highway. He gets water from Seville, but he's got the stream, too. He has diesel generators and pumps, and a tank to store water for dry times."

It's easy to see what Takigawa is worried about. The banks of the stream are raised. That elevation gives shooters at the tree line an advantage over men in the field. A dirt road runs along the stream and branches off to the garage at the back of the ranch. A pipe aqueduct runs from the stream to a pump house, and up to the water tower.

"We need someone on this side," I say. "It'll be tough to cover at night."

"Depending on the light. A full moon will help. If we get a new moon, forget it."

"Full moon was three days ago."

"That'll be enough."

We walk past the *cuadrilla's* bunkhouse and stroll down to the garage. Look inside at the vast collection of ranch and farm equipment, caravans, SUVs, and luxury cars. Rincón's Mercedes has been freshly washed. A few feet away, a ranch hand is polishing a breathtaking 1930 Maybach Zeppelin V12 cruiser. A collector's piece from the Spanish Civil War.

I whistle. "Wonder if the maestro's family was friends with the generalissimo."

"Fighting bulls must pay well."

We stroll over to the Maybach Zeppelin. I greet the ranch hand. *"Buenos dias. ¿Habla Inglés?"*

"A little, señor."

"Does the maestro drive this car, or watch you polish it with a diaper?"

The man laughs. "The maestro drives it on country roads. He never drives it in town."

"Has he had it long?"

"All his life, señor. It belonged to his father."

We leave the garage through a side door and walk back to the Big House. On the way, we pass Fernando's cook-house. The door is open, and we hear the crackle of frying grease. The aroma of freshly cooked food signals lunch is on the way.

The windows on the west side of the house face the mountains. Plantation shutters protect them from the sun. I count the windows—the kitchen, the dining hall, the living

room. The library lies on the east side and looks onto the
driveway.

Herders on horseback dot the fields. They are distinctive
in their flat-topped, wide-brimmed gaucho hats. They all
carry lances.

"The three of us can't be up all night," Takigawa says.

"No. Three watches, and we draw straws. You, me and
Ballard. When Heth isn't with Julia, she'll swap out with
Ballard. We have three Z84s, and we'll have nine ranch
hands who can use them. That makes three watches of four
men each—three hands, and one of us. One man at each
point of the compass."

"What kind of strength does the enemy have?" Takigawa
asks.

"I haven't seen either group attack with more than four
men. But that doesn't mean they can't. Stein tells me both
The Basque and Leandro have operations that span France
and Spain."

Takigawa shrugs. "Stein won't have us sitting on Princess
Julia for long. I bet she'll have us extract the package in no
time."

"That would be good. I'd love to get back to my
vacation."

"LET'S get it over with, Breed."

Heth walks toward me, the AR-15 slung over her shoulder. She's wearing yellow-tinted mil-spec shooting glasses
and her ten-gallon hat.

I check my watch. "This shouldn't take long."

After Ballard went to swap duty with Heth, I carried two
posts to the bullring. Outside the ring, with open space

behind, I planted one post a hundred yards out and another twenty-five yards out. I drew circles on two pieces of paper and pinned them to the posts.

"Zero at a hundred yards," I tell her. "91.4 meters."

Heth unslings the AR-15 and deploys the bipod. She lies prone, sets up the rifle, and focuses on the target at twenty-five yards.

Crack.

"I'm on paper."

Heth licks her lips. Adjusts the knobs on the scope, dials in her corrections. She doesn't bother firing a second shot at twenty-five. The Steiner is an excellent optic. The elevation and windage turrets are rugged, reliable, and accurate.

"I'm going out to a hundred," she says.

That's confidence. Heth settles in for her first shot at a hundred yards. Slowly squeezes the trigger.

Crack.

It's hard for me to be sure without binoculars. "Are you on paper?"

"Yes." Heth squints, counts the marks on her reticle. She's measuring the horizontal and vertical distance of her point-of-impact from the bull's-eye. "I have to adjust for burn rate."

Seville is hot. Under these conditions, the powder in Heth's ammunition burns faster. It generates a higher muzzle velocity.

"Right point-seven-five," Heth mutters to herself, adjusting the windage. "Down six."

I remain silent.

Heth takes a breath, lets half of it out, squeezes the trigger.

Crack.

The paper jerks with the impact and the post splinters. Heth gets to her feet and unloads the AR-15.

"Want to go over and check it out?" I ask.

Heth shakes her head, slings the rifle, and pushes her glasses up on the bridge of her nose. "No. We're golden."

25

Heth and I step out of the cool interior of the Big House. We've left Ballard and Julia sitting in the kitchen, drinking coffee. They promised to join us later. I think Julia is reluctant to go out in the heat. The sun has passed its zenith, but it's still burning. Heth's ten-gallon hat provides protection from the sun. I'm bare-headed, and I know I'll suffer later.

"How long before we ditch the princess?" Heth asks.

"I don't know. Stein is still negotiating with the State Department."

Rincón stands at the outer fence of the bullring. Vaqueros are sitting on the fence, or leaning against the *barrera*. "Hello, Ms Crockett." The matador flashes Heth a broad smile. "Are you ready for your first lesson?"

"Yes, Maestro. Please call me Heth."

"Thank you, Heth. You may call me Javier, if you wish."

"Yes, Maestro."

Allegre is standing at the gate with a ten-year-old boy. The picador hands a red *muleta* to Rincón. The little boy is holding a pair of bull's horns mounted on a stick. He beams at Heth.

Rincón opens the gate. He takes Heth by the elbow. "Come inside the *ruedo*."

Heth follows the matador into the ring. The little boy follows them with the stick and horns.

"This is Pepe," Rincón says. "He will help you learn your passes."

The matador stands ten feet from the boy, with his feet together and the red cape held before his body. "Pepe will act as a bull," Rincón says. "He will charge at your *muleta*. Your role is to distract him with the cape and avoid his horns. It is necessary for you to learn these passes before you face a bull."

Rincón holds the cape in front of him and twitches it. "*¡Hoy! ¡Toro!*"

The boy holds the horns to his head, bends at the hips, and charges the cape. It is the most innocent child's game one can imagine—a boy pretending to be a bull. Rincón moves the cape to one side. The boy follows it and passes harmlessly by the matador.

"That," Rincón says, "is a *verónica*. It is the simplest pass. Many people think the matador must move his body to avoid the bull. No. The matador guides the bull with the *muleta*. He guides the bull *away* from his body."

"It's so graceful," Heth says.

"Heth, the *corrida* is only a fight in a superficial sense. In the end, it is an art, and the *torero* is a performer. Now, you try."

Rincón shows Heth how to hold the *muleta*. She stands in front of the boy, the cape held before her. Flaps the cloth.

Before she can react, Pepe charges. Heth freezes and the

boy runs into her with the horns. Heth cries out and stumbles backward. Rincón and the vaqueros sitting on the fence laugh.

"You must move the cape," Rincón says. "Pepe is behaving exactly as a bull will behave. The bull is nearsighted. All he sees is a blur where you stand, and a patch of red. You must deflect him with the *muleta*. Now try again."

Ballard and Julia join us. Ballard carries his M4 on a two-point sling, muzzle down. Julia leans on the *barrera* next to me. Her elbow touches mine.

"*Toro.*"

Pepe lowers his head and comes at Heth a second time. Heth waits till the last moment, shifts the *muleta* to one side. Pepe follows the cape with his horns and brushes Heth's hip.

"*¡Olé!*" The vaqueros clap.

Rincón tilts his head, appraises Heth.

"*Excellent*," he says. "Now. Let me show you the *gaonera.*"

RINCÓN MAKES Heth practice the passes with Pepe for half an hour. The *verónica*, with the cape held in front of the matador, and the *gaonera*, with the cape held to one side and behind, in a graceful turning motion. The latter appears more dangerous, because the *torero* exposes his body to the bull instead of concealing it behind the cape.

"*Excellent*," Rincón says. "That is enough for now, Heth. Why don't you rest."

Flushed, Heth thanks Pepe and returns the *muleta* to Rincón. She joins us at the *barrera*. "That was cool," she says. "When do you think I can try a real bull?"

Rincón smiles, nods to Allegre.

A ranch hand carrying a long lance leads a fine Arabian

horse into the *ruedo*. The horse wears padded body armor.
Allegre mounts the horse and takes the lance. It is made of
pine, with a sharp point and a crossbar, called the *cruceta*.
The crossbar is four inches from the point. It prevents the
lance from penetrating too deeply.

"That man, Allegre, is a picador," I say. "His lance is
called a pic. In a *corrida*, it is used to weaken the bull."

One of Rincón's *peóns* enters the ring. Ranch hands open
a gate, and a bull charges into the ring. It's a small bull, but
fast and frisky. The ranch hand closes the gate and ducks
behind the *barrera*.

The *peón* darts to the center of the ring, between the bull
and Allegre. Waves a pink and yellow cape at the bull. The
bull jerks its head toward the *peón* and charges.

"Why isn't that cape red?" Heth asks.

"That is a *capote de brega*," Rincón says "A work cape. The
bull is a *vaquilla*, a young calf. Allegre is going to test her for
bravery."

"Her?" Julia sounds surprised.

"We do not expose male calves to the cape, nor to men
on foot. As I said, it is against the law. In practice, male calves
learn too quickly. They remember too much and will
become impossible to work with as they grow older."

The *peón* performs a *verónica* pass, then dodges behind
the cover of the *barrera*. The *vaquilla* snorts, paws the earth,
and charges Allegre's horse. It rams the body armor, and the
picador uses his lance to ward off the bull. The calf backs off,
charges again.

"This is a good calf," Rincón says. "A brave calf will
charge anything that moves. She will be good for breeding."

The *vaquilla* charges Allegre's horse again and again. The
picador has to work to keep the calf under control.

Rincón draws a Havana from the breast pocket of his *chaleco*. Slices it and lights up. "Heth."

"Yes, Maestro?"

"Go out and do some *verónicas*."

I meet Rincón's eyes with a sharp glance. Does he know what he's doing? That calf may not be full grown, but she has a pair of sharp horns. She's a good five hundred pounds, and aggressive as hell. Is Heth ready after thirty minutes of lessons?

Rincón shifts his cool gaze to Heth. Never one to back down, Heth takes the *muleta* from the matador and steps into the ring.

The picador canters away from the calf, leaving it to face Heth. She steps forward and meets the animal in the center of the *ruedo*. Holds the cape in front of her.

Carrying his work cape, the *peón* steps into the ring. He's anxious, prepared to intervene. Allegre stands with his horse at the *barrera*.

"*Toro.*"

The calf paws the dirt. Charges Heth at a full gallop. Heth waits till the last second, moves the *muleta* fractionally to her right. The calf buries its head and horns in the cape. Heth snaps the cloth over its body like a fluttering flag. The calf misses her by an inch.

"*¡Ole!*" The vaqueros cheer.

Julia squeezes my forearm.

Rincón looks at me sideways. Calmly draws cigar smoke into his lungs, exhales luxuriously.

The calf, carried by its momentum, skids to a stop and whirls around. Finds Heth standing in front of it, *muleta* spread.

Heth jerks the cloth. Attracted by the movement, the calf

charges a second time. Again, Heth shifts the *muleta* and the calf misses her by an inch. Twice more, the calf skids to a stop, whirls, and charges Heth. Each time, she deflects the calf's attention with the cape. The vaqueros cheer every pass. "¡*Ole!*"

Each time, however, the calf's turning circle tightens. With every pass, Heth has less time to prepare. On the fifth pass, the calf brushes her hip.

The sixth pass is tight. Heth moves the cape further to give herself room, but the calf's shoulder hits her right thigh. She's knocked off balance and loses her grip on the *muleta*. The calf's horns tangle in the cape and rip it out of her hands. Heth falls sideways, hits the ground, and scrambles to her feet.

In a flash, the *peón* darts between Heth and the calf. Draws the animal away from the girl by waving his work cape.

Heth runs and ducks behind the *barrera* next to Rincón. "Oh my God."

"Are you alright?" I ask.

"Yes." Heth looks at Rincón. "Maestro, that was *great*. Can we do it again?"

Rincón puffs on his cigar and smiles.

26

RANCHO RINCÓN – FRIDAY, EVENING

S leep when you can, eat when you can. I go to bed early, but I'm too tired to sleep. I drift in and out. The sound of footsteps shuffling in the hall wakes me. My watch tells me it's almost ten o'clock. I reach for the Mark 23 on the table. Get up, put on my shoes, and open my door.

M4 across his knees, Ballard is sitting on the floor outside Julia's room. He's eating a sandwich, drinking a glass of orange juice, and reading from his phone's browser. I let out a breath and slip the Mark 23 under my shirt.

"What's up?" I ask.

"Heth's gone downstairs," Ballard says. "I'm watching the princess."

Takigawa is on the perimeter, with three of Rincón's ranch hands. I walk down the grand staircase. The polished mahogany surface is smooth under my palm. I push open the door to the library. Heth is curled up on the sofa, reading an old book on bullfighting. It's big and heavy, with eight-by-ten-inch black-and-white photographs of matadors in the ring.

Heth looks up when I enter. "Breed, this was the most exciting day of my life. Bullfighting beats barrel racing hands down."

"I'm glad you had fun."

"I am so glad I came. Thanks for asking me."

Heth leans her head back against the sofa. She looks around the library at the paintings of matadors, the bulls' heads mounted on the walls. "Breed, when that bull charges, you feel alive. I want to do it with a fully grown bull. When we get home, if I have to go to Mexico to do it, I will."

I walk to an easy chair and sit down opposite Heth.

"Does it mean that much to you?"

"It does." Heth smiles. "We'll watch the maestro perform this weekend, won't we?"

A full-length portrait on the wall catches my eye. It's a portrait of Rincón, dressed in his *traje de luces*—his suit of lights, the traditional bullfighter's costume.

"I don't know what Stein will want to do with Julia. She could be shipped out tomorrow. Whatever happens, I promise you'll get to watch the *corrida*."

Heth sets the book aside, rises from the sofa, and bends to hug me. "Stay with me to see it?"

I'm surprised by the emotion in Heth's voice. It's not like the childish flirting we've enjoyed all our lives.

Crack!

That's the sound of an M4 firing. More gunshots follow the first.

Heth straightens, and I leap to my feet. The shots are coming from the Big House's front porch. We're under attack.

. . .

HETH and I run to the front door.

Takigawa is on the porch, next to one of the stone pillars. He's firing from a kneeling position. Pounding rounds into the windshield of a black Mercedes SUV roaring toward the house. We're pinned by the glare of its headlights. Two more SUVs follow close behind, lights off.

The SUVs are coming straight down the drive from the highway. Blacked out, they approached quietly. When Takigawa started shooting, the lead car threw its headlights on to blind him.

There's a crackle of automatic fire. Muzzle flashes sparkle from the front compartment of the SUV. A man sitting in the passenger seat is firing straight through the windshield.

Firing through a windshield is difficult with a small-caliber weapon. Low-velocity pistol and submachine gun rounds deflect. Until you make a hole big enough to fire through, your gunfire is inaccurate.

Takigawa hits the driver, and the vehicle fishtails. Three feet from the porch, it slews sideways and lurches to a stop. Rocks on its suspension. Three men jump out of the vehicle. One from the front passenger seat, two from the rear passenger compartment. They're carrying H&K MP5s. Takigawa shoots the first man in the chest. The gunman pitches backwards and drops his weapon. The other two dodge behind the vehicle.

Heth and I instinctively throw ourselves prone behind one of the stone pillars. I level my Mark 23 and shoot out the headlights of the first car. The two other SUVs flick their lights on. Heth fires her BM and shoots those out too.

The driver of the second SUV floors the accelerator and rams the porch. The front of the vehicle jumps the steps. Takigawa seeks cover behind the stone pillar to the left. Heth and I are prone behind the stone pillar to the right. Takigawa fires his M4 into the windshield at point-blank range. The driver and the front passenger jerk with the impact of Takigawa's bullets.

A man spills out of the left rear passenger seat, and I shoot him in the chest. Another dismounts from the right rear passenger seat and Takigawa shoots him in the face. The third vehicle screeches to a halt behind the first two. Men jump out and turn weapons on us. The muzzle flashes from their submachine guns twinkle. Bullets whine off the stone pillars and slam into the wooden front of the Big House.

There's a boom and a blast of rock chips flies from the stone pillar. One of the men from the third SUV has a double-barreled shotgun. I watch him break it and fish two more shells from his jacket pocket. He reloads, points it in our general direction, and fires a second time.

Rincón's ranch hands come running. They turn their Z84 submachine guns on the vehicles. One man fires from the south corner of the Big House. Another, who had been on watch at the garage, is firing from between the *cuadrilla's* and the ranch hands' bunkhouses. The third man fires from between the bullpens and the stables.

The attackers don't know how to fire submachine guns. They like to do mag dumps on full auto. Submachine guns are difficult to control. Their bullets riddle the front of the Big House above our heads.

Ballard's training of Rincón's men is paying off. The ranch hands squeeze the Z84 stocks against their shoulders and fire short, controlled bursts. After each burst, they correct their aim.

The man with the shotgun shouts commands to the others. The two men from the first SUV run to the third, open the hatchback, and throw themselves inside. The other men get into the car. The driver shifts the vehicle into reverse and floors the gas. The SUV leaps backward.

I get to my feet. Takigawa and I advance, firing. The rear window of the SUV shatters. The vehicle speeds toward the highway and disappears.

The two other SUVs are a shambles. One sits, stopped at an angle in front of the porch. The other has been driven halfway up the steps. Their windows are shattered, and their headlights have been shot out. All their doors hang open. Bodies are either slumped inside, sprawled on the ground, or hanging out of the vehicles. Blood has splattered every-where and is pooling under the bodies.

Heth reacted well under fire. Helped me shoot out the SUVs' headlights. I don't think she shot any of the gunmen.

I turn to Heth. "Go upstairs. Wait with Julia and Ballard."

Takigawa clears the left side of the vehicles, I clear the right. All but one of the men we shot are dead.

The wounded man is barely conscious. He's been hit several times in the chest. Took several rounds from Taki-gawa's M4 and my Mark 23.

"Who do you work for?" I ask.

The man's eyes close. We're losing him.

Takigawa applies CPR. Kneels next to the man and begins chest compressions. With every thrust, blood splashes Takigawa's forearms and spurts from exit wounds in the man's back. It's like pumping on a bullet-riddled waterbed. A black pool spreads under the body. I get to my feet and step back.

Ranch hands have gathered in a circle around us. Three of them carry Z84s, low ready.

"He's gone." My mouth fills with a sour taste. "Leave him alone."

Takigawa gets up. His jeans are soaked at the knees.

"That was fucked up," he says.

My phone buzzes. It's Heth.

"Breed, you'd better get up here."

27

I climb the porch steps. Bang through the front door and take the grand staircase two steps at a time. Rincón and Heth stand at the landing, staring at Ballard. Throat slashed, the Echo is lying on his back. A small greeting card envelope lies on his chest.

"He is dead," Rincón says. "We found him like this."

"Julia's gone," Heth says.

The envelope isn't sealed. I pick it up and slide a piece of paper from inside. The message has been printed in English:

WE HAVE THE GIRL. YOU WILL BE CONTACTED.

I hand the note to Heth. Step inside Julia's room. It's empty. I check the windows. They're shuttered, but that doesn't matter. They overlook the massacre on the drive. We would have seen or heard anyone jumping onto the porch roof.

I bend down and close Ballard's eyes. "Who found him?"

"I did," Heth says.

Rincón presses his palm to his chest. "I was in my room, watching the battle from my window. I came out when Heth screamed."

Heth blushes. "I freaked out."

I take out my phone and punch Takigawa's speed dial.

"We lost the package," I say. "Have you got the ranch hands back at their posts?"

"Affirmative. We're secure."

"Watch the front. I need to find out what happened."

There are no obvious signs of a struggle in the girls' room. Then again, Julia isn't a strong girl. She's Heth's height, but a good twenty pounds lighter. Weakened by the ordeal of withdrawal.

I pick up Ballard's M4 and check it. The weapon is charged and safe. It has not been fired.

"He heard the gunshots," I say. "Charged his weapon, but kept it safe. Stayed at Julia's door."

I open the door to my room and look inside. The space is undisturbed, the shutters fastened from within. They overlook the garage, the bunkhouses, and the stream. I step back into the hall and go to Rincón's bedroom. Open the door and enter without permission.

The master bedroom is enormous. And empty. King-sized bed. Walk-in closet, also empty. Full-length mirrors to satisfy a vain aristocrat. Windows on three sides. The ones facing west and north are shuttered. The ones overlooking the porch are also closed, except for the window at the corner.

Rincón is telling the truth. He heard the shooting. Went to the corner and opened one window to peep out. Wanted to see what was going on, didn't want to expose himself to gunfire. No one came through here.

My phone buzzes. It's Takigawa.

"What's up?" I ask.

"They broke into the garage. Stole a pickup."

"Swap with a ranch hand. Meet us out back."

I hand Heth her AR-15 and go down the stairs. Rincón and Heth follow me to the kitchen. This was where the killer entered the house. He broke in while the frontal attack distracted us. He went up the stairs and killed Ballard. Then he disabled Julia, took her downstairs, and left the way he came. Stole a pickup and made good his escape.

The kitchen door has been forced. The same crude technique Leandro's men used on Rincón's hotel room.

Rincón flicks a switch and a light comes on over the kitchen door. Its glow illuminates the path to the cookhouse and garage. Takigawa is waiting for us. He raises his hand in acknowledgment.

"You getting a picture?" Takigawa asks.

"It's not perfect, but things are falling into place."

There's a ranch hand with a submachine gun inside the garage. He shows us an empty parking space next to the waxed Maybach Zeppelin. Only this morning, Takigawa and I stood here, admiring the vintage automobile.

The blue Volkswagen pickup is gone.

"The frontal attack was a decoy," Takigawa says, "and it was well coordinated. A vehicle unloaded the kidnapper a mile away and he approached on foot."

The garage is so large it has five separate garage doors. All have dedicated tracks, rollers and motors. The one in front of the Mercedes, Maybach Zeppelin, and the empty space for the missing blue pickup stands wide open.

I point to the tree line. "He followed the road that runs

by the stream. In the moonlight, he wouldn't stand out against the trees."

"Yes." Takigawa says. "He could have walked upright. Without night vision or thermals, no one would spot him. He stopped at the pipe aqueduct. Got on his belly, crawled two hundred yards to the house."

"Using the aqueduct as cover."

"He waited until his friends launched the decoy attack. Only then, when our sentry left his post, did he break cover and run to the house."

I'm kicking myself. This is what happens when you try to provide personal protection with an ad hoc force. A proper security detail wouldn't have been caught out. We would have had more men, appropriately armed. We would have had night vision and squad radios. Most importantly, the men would have all been trained professionals. They wouldn't have left their posts.

"We have six new MP5s," I say. "Let's give them to the rest of our men."

Rincón's brow furrows. "Do you think they will attack again?"

"Let's not take chances." I turn to Heth. "Keep your rifle with you at all times. Pick up some ammo and reload your pistol mag."

My phone buzzes. I take it out of my pocket. I'm not looking forward to speaking with Stein.

No need to worry. It's an unknown number. I hit the send button. "Breed."

Leandro speaks English with a pronounced Spanish accent. There's an insolence to his tone. "Breed," he says. "You have handled my property all week. That is going to cost you."

"Julia's not your property."

"You think not? I can do what I want to her. Did you enjoy breaking her of the habit? Were you tempted? I'm sure you could not resist."

The gypsy describes Julia submitting to acts so vile they are beyond my imagination.

"The girl has skills, Breed. I taught her myself. One injection, and she will be as you found her. Do you want me to do that?"

I want to kill him, that's what I want. Stick the Mark 23 in his mouth and pull the trigger. I say nothing.

"It might please me to do so anyway. I should enjoy her one last time before throwing her away like soiled tissue. Do you want her back? Have thirty million Euros ready by tomorrow evening. I will contact you again."

Leandro disconnects the call.

Rincón, Takigawa and Heth stare at me.

"Who was that?" Heth asks.

"The Gypsy King. He has Julia, and he wants thirty million Euros for her. By tomorrow night."

Takigawa strokes his beard. "Will Stein pay?"

"We're going to find out."

I WALK AWAY from the group. Suck in the warm Andalusian air. This late at night, it's still warm. It won't cool off for another couple hours. I hit Stein's speed dial.

"Breed, I don't have any news for you. State can't make up their minds. I couldn't take it anymore. Left them doing a circle-jerk."

"Unfortunately, I have news for *you*. We've lost the package."

I tell Stein what happened. No sugar-coating, no wasted words, no recriminations. This was not a full-on exec protect. I couldn't ask her to send me a full detail. We operated on a shoestring. Now we've lost a man, and we have to deal with it.

"I'll try to get the money for you," Stein says. "Maybe this will focus State's attention."

"There's one more thing you can do for me."

"What's that?"

"Leandro called me to deliver the ransom demand. And rub shit in my face."

"So?"

"You have my number. You can trace the source of that call. Get me that, and Takigawa and I will return his surprise."

"*That*, I can do."

"Let me know."

28

RANCHO RINCÓN – SATURDAY, EARLY MORNING

Rincón and Salazar busy themselves organizing a cleanup of the ranch. I want to tell the maestro I'm sorry for the bullet holes in his stone pillars and timber walls. Can't bring myself to do it. It would be a useless gesture, and I have a dead operator. What's a few bullet holes compared to a human life?

I walk with Takigawa and Heth back to the drive. We watch Rincón's men tow the attackers' SUVs to the garage. Rancho Rincón has refrigerated storage. It's located in the barn that houses the stables and cow pens. Ballard and the dead gypsies are carried there and folded into tarps.

"Think we can find that phone?" Takigawa reloads his M4. Takes the partially emptied magazine and drops it into a haversack.

"We'll find the phone," I say. "The question is, what will be on the other end?"

"You think it's a burner?"

"Could be. But we have to go with what we've got."

"I guess you're right. What about The Basque and
Colonel Orlov?"

"They're out there. Probably saw the whole thing.
Watched Leandro drive away in his little blue pickup. They
figure he has Julia, and they're trying to figure out how to
find her."

"How can they find her?"

"Orlov has the same geolocation technology we do. He
also has hooks into the Spanish police, just like us. He'll get
Russian military intelligence—the GRU—to work its
contacts. Pull the license plate of Rincón's pickup, get the
cops to watch for it."

"Russia can get the Spanish police to search for Julia?"

"The Spanish police don't even need to know it's Russia
asking. Money talks."

"What about The Basque?"

"Same thing. We already know his organization operates
with impunity in Spain. That can only be because he has the
police in his pocket."

Takigawa grunts. "Wait till the police get the same
request from three different sources."

"They'll sell the information three times over."

"If Stein comes through, she'll send us right to Leandro,"
Heth says.

"Not if Leandro's ditched a burner. If it is a burner, everything depends on how long he holds on to it. Just to make
life interesting, Orlov and The Basque have another way to
find Leandro."

"What's that?"

"They can follow *us*."

"Can you believe Ballard didn't get off a shot?" Takigawa
asks.

"No. But I can't see how they took him out. We don't know how many men entered the house. It's possible Ballard knew one or more of the men who killed him."

Heth stares at me. "Who?"

"Ballard trained nine of Rincón's men to use Z84s. That alone would develop a sense of familiarity."

Takigawa frowns. "What about Rincón?"

"You have a suspicious nature."

"It's the ninja in me. Again, what about Rincón?"

"He claims he watched the battle from his window. I checked out his bedroom—a shutter overlooking the porch was open. He wasn't lying about *that*."

"Didn't he hear any noise from the hall?"

"Apparently not. There was a lot of shooting, and Ballard was killed with a knife. I'm not sure there was any noise for the maestro to hear."

"No one is missing from the ranch," Takigawa says.

"That means Leandro's confederate is still here."

"We're in trouble." Heth pulls an elastic band from her wrist and binds her hair back in a ponytail.

"It doesn't matter," I say. "Our priority is to find Julia. We don't need Rincón's people for that."

"I don't like any of this."

"Neither do I. From now on, we stick together."

"WE'VE TRACED THE CALL," Stein says. "I'll message you the address."

"Thanks, Stein. We'll move on them as soon as we can."

"You know there is no guarantee they'll be there."

"Understood. If it's a burner, it all depends on whether he's still got it. We have to move fast."

"Either way, I'm bringing the ransom. I'll be arriving at
Morón at noon your time."

"We'll meet you."

"Let's hope you free her before I get there."

TAKIGAWA AND HETH sit on either side of me on the sofa.
We're in the library, and I'm searching for the address on
Magellan Navigator. Magellan is a powerful phone applica-
tion. The software integrates satellite imagery, photographic
databases, and imaging software. It creates realistic three-
dimensional maps and models of any location on the planet.

I'm having trouble finding the address on Magellan.
"Where *is* this place?"

"The bullring and the Seville cathedral stand out on the
map." Heth points to an oval structure. "There it is, east of
the bullring, north of the cathedral. Less than half a mile."

The streets between the bullring and the target are a
disorganized jumble of alleys and lanes. "It's a rabbit warren.
I don't know how accurate the GPS maps are, but once we're
in there it could take an hour to find it."

"It must be the old town," Heth says. "Hundreds of years
old. They might have redone some buildings but didn't
change the street plan."

I rotate the image. Examine it in three dimensions, from
all four points of the compass. "Look, here's the river and the
Maestranza—the bullring. The cathedral is south-by-east.
The fastest approach is by the river highway, but at some
point we're going to have to go into the city."

I forward the address to Heth and Takigawa. "Bookmark
it. Let's hit the road, study it on the way."

We get up and find Rincón in the living room. He's sitting

with Salazar, discussing the disposal of Leandro's SUVs and the bodies of his men. They are going to stuff the bodies in the vehicles and push them into a secluded stretch of the Guadalquivir.

"We'll return our friend to America," I tell him. "There will be an airplane to pick up his casket."

"We have no casket. Ordering one will appear suspicious."

"We will take care of everything at Morón. There will be a casket, packed with ice, and a flag."

"Of course," Rincón says. "He was a veteran, yes? Have no fear. We will keep him for you."

Salazar crosses himself.

I ask for permission to borrow one of Rincón's Volkswagen pickup trucks.

"By all means, take either one. But the sun is not yet up. Where are you going?"

"We're going to look for Julia," I tell him. "The sun will be up by the time we reach Seville. We'll be gone most of the day."

"That is alright," Rincón says. "My *cuadrilla* must prepare for tomorrow's *corrida*."

"In that case, we'll get out of your way."

"Before I forget." The low coffee table in front of the sofa is intricately carved mahogany. Rincón pulls open a drawer and takes out an envelope. Hands it to Heth. "These are tickets to the *corrida* tomorrow. The best in all the *Maestranza*. For you and your friends."

Heth glows. "Thank you, Maestro."

We go upstairs and pack our duffels with weapons and ammunition. From under my bed, I take a cardboard box. It's packed with cloth and the four remaining perfume bottles. I

call Takigawa and Heth into my room and show them the
IEDs.

Takigawa grunts. "How reactive is it?"

"Not as reactive as nitro, but I wouldn't play catch. We'll
take them along. Keep them padded, in an air-conditioned
environment."

"Drive carefully. We get in a car crash, there won't be
enough of us left to bury."

I pack the bottles into a small vinyl carrying case.
Swaddle them in face towels to prevent bumping. When I'm
done, the bottles sit in a cozy, shock-proof cocoon.

"You got one of these?" I ask Takigawa. My shaving kit is
in a six-inch zippered overnight case with a short carry
handle on one end. I shake the toiletries out, put them in a
plastic bag, and undo my belt. Slide the tongue through the
case's carry handle and buckle up. Now I can put one bottle
in the toiletry case, zip it, and keep my hands free to handle
a weapon.

"Damn, you are so organized," Takigawa says. "No, I
don't."

I look at Heth.

"Nope. Sorry."

We sling our duffels over our shoulders and carry them
to the garage. I carry the case with the IEDs in my right
hand. The air smells hot. To the east, the sky is lightening, a
hint of the blazing sunrise to come. The mountains to the
north and west remain dark blue humps. Their peaks have
yet to be touched by sunlight. The tree line that borders the
stream looks black and ominous.

The buildings of Rancho Rincón are dark. This place is a
tight community. I think of Salazar, Fernando, and Carmen.
All the ranch hands. Two of them were killed on the road,

and they watched us kill six more men in front of the Big House last night. They are all loyal to Rincón, and not one of them will say a word. They're like a family, and the matador is their Godfather.

And yet. I am convinced one of them betrayed us last night. One of them was with Leandro when he killed Ballard.

Salazar lets us into the garage. He turns on the lights and leads us to the pickups. He gives us the keys to one and touches a button on a garage door opener. The motor hums and the metal panels of the door are drawn up on their rollers.

I can't stop thinking about the attack. Modern vehicles are difficult to hotwire. Somebody gave Leandro the keys to the pickup.

"The tank is full," the old man says, "and there are many petrol stations along the way."

"Thank you, señor."

"You are going to bring back the girl?"

"Yes. And kill the men who took her."

"*Vaya con Dios.*"

29

SEVILLE – SATURDAY, MORNING

The road stretches before us. We drive west, away from the rising sun and into the darkness. Takigawa sits on my right. Heth sits on the bench behind us. Our rifles and ammunition are in duffel bags on the floor. The vinyl bag containing the IEDs lies tucked between Heth's feet.

I think of the Gypsy King and his men. They'll kill Julia whether we pay them or not. We have to kill them first.

The disc of the sun is peeping above the horizon in my rearview mirror. I've got the pickup's air conditioner running full blast and the cab is chilly. I follow the signs that lead to the river. The Guadalquivir appears on the left. In the half-light, it's a glossy, serpentine green. Under a blue sky, the waters will shine aquamarine.

I check the rearview mirror. Glance left and right at the cars around me to see if we're being followed. It's harder than I expected, despite the light traffic. The glare of the sun makes my rearview mirror useless. A professional team will rotate their vehicles, taking turns in the tail position. I'm sure Orlov called for support as soon as he confirmed Julia's presence. The Basque has his whole organization to draw from.

The river curves gently to the left. We drive past medieval wharves. Centuries-old masonry and timber. Columbus set sail from here, on his way to the New World. A continent that would become America.

Ahead, in the distance, is a low, white wall. The *Maestranza*, the oldest and most beautiful bullring in the world. I point it out to Heth.

"That's where we're going tomorrow?" Heth asks.

"Yes. It's the spiritual heart of bullfighting, and the crowds are the most demanding."

My eye travels to the right. There, to the east, rises the golden spire of the Giralda. The structure, once the minaret of a 12th Century mosque, was converted after the reconquest. Once, a muezzin would climb the Giralda to issue the Muslim call to prayer. Today, it's the bell tower of Seville's cathedral.

Takigawa squints at his phone, manipulates the Magellan Navigator.

"I've got a route," he says. "It's more distance, but it's quicker. There is no straight line through there."

Takigawa guides me right, onto Avenue Menéndez de Pelayo. We leave the river behind. Its benches, with views of the water and early morning joggers. Now is the time to get that run in. Before the life-threatening heat becomes overwhelming.

The avenue runs straight north-by-east. We pass wooden bleachers set up for people to watch the processions. Seats and streets are still covered with litter from the Good Friday parades. Some revelers are slumped where they fell asleep. Street sweepers work around them. Why bother? This evening they'll party on.

God, what a devastated piece of territory. I'd studied Seville with an eye to my vacation. Every square foot of this city is drenched in history.

We pass the Real Alcázar, the palace built by King Peter the Cruel. The Catholic monarch was named, and later excommunicated, for his persecution of the clergy. He helped the Sultan of Granada resist Catholic invasions.

Takigawa chose our route well. It's a wide street, unusual for Santa Cruz. This is the *barrio*, the oldest district of Seville, and once the poorest. It's a place of narrow streets, dark alleys, and tiny cobblestone squares.

"Left rudder," Takigawa says.

"Shit." I pull off the avenue. Right away we find ourselves in a narrow street, blocked by street sweepers, early-rising tourists, and a group of teenagers carrying musical instruments. They are hurrying to a morning rehearsal. They'll perform at processions in the afternoon. I nose ahead, reluctant to lean on the horn.

"If we're still here two hours from now," Heth says, "we'll never get out."

"That's Iglesia El Salvador." Takigawa points at a church. "The landmark I've been looking for."

I've read about El Salvador, too. That church was once Seville's mosque. I think of the war we are fighting against militant Islam. Wonder if some day they'll convert these churches back to mosques. I push the thought from my mind.

"There it is," Takigawa says. "*Veinticinco.*"

Number 25. It's a two-story building, with a pharmacy on
the ground floor. Still closed. The front of the pharmacy is
protected by accordion security gates. The wings of the gates
are drawn across the front of the shop from either side.
Where they meet is a hasp to which a heavy padlock has
been fitted.

I drive past, go around the block. It's not a block as *we*
think of it in America. The little streets in the *barrio* are not
arranged in straight lines. In America you have four streets
arranged at right angles to each other. Here you have five
arranged at odd angles. The block is a pentagon of claustro-
phobic alleys and lanes.

Ten feet from the end of the alley, I stop the pickup. The
pickup is pointed straight at the target building. That gives
us a clear view.

To the left of the accordion gate is a recessed alcove and a
wooden door. The number 25A, in faded white paint, is
barely visible. A dollar gets you ten it leads to narrow stairs
that lead to the second floor. The second floor windows are
shuttered.

Metal fire stairs have been bolted to the right side of the
building. There is a landing next to a door and a shuttered
window.

"Single unit or multiple?" Takigawa asks.

"Single. There's only one unit number—25A."

"Think there's a way to reach the second floor from the
back?"

"We can't afford to guess wrong. Heth, get behind the
wheel."

Heth switches places with me. I walk back the way we
came, reverse the route I drove around the block. It wouldn't
do for anyone following us to see me emerge from our little

alley. They would know right away where our vehicle is parked.

The narrow streets are not far removed from nineteenth-century squalor. Windows have been opened to ventilate cramped cells. Apartments are warmer at night than they are during the day, because they hold in the heat. From one open window, I hear a toilet flush. From another comes the sound of bodies bouncing on an old mattress and rusty bedsprings.

I walk past the pharmacy. My eyes sweep the street for anything unusual. I've created a problem for anybody following us. They'd have to either stop well back, or pass us. That's hard to do in streets this narrow.

A surveillance team would do the latter. The primary would pass us, radio our position to his secondary, and disappear. The secondary would stop several blocks away, but within visual range. The tertiary would also stop, far enough away for us not to see him.

I've lost the primary. He doesn't know where we've gone. If he searches for us, we'll identify him. All he knows is that we're interested in the street we passed. So when I pulled around the block, he kept going and had his secondary stop to keep watch.

There they are. A silver four-door Citroën sedan. Two men in front.

Who are they? Russian or Basque?

Those aren't Basque haircuts. But that doesn't mean there aren't Basques around.

I walk around the pharmacy, past the fire stairs. They're painted black, bleeding brown rust. At the end of the building, I turn left. There's a back entrance to the pharmacy, protected by a portcullis and a massive padlock.

The windows on the second floor are shuttered.

I make my way back to the pickup by a roundabout route.

"What's it like?" Takigawa asks.

Heth is behind the wheel, so I get in the back seat. Take a pad of paper and a pen from my duffel, sketch the building. "That's it," I tell him. "The fire escape is exposed to the street. That door next to the pharmacy leads to the second floor. There's probably another locked door at the top of a staircase."

"But," Takigawa says, "the front door at the top can't be seen from the street."

"Exactly. That's our most direct way in. Also, I don't like the idea of splitting up. We don't know what the interior layout is like."

"Two is one, one is none. We both go through the front door."

"There are two men in a silver Citroën twenty yards down the street," I tell him.

"Orlov?"

"The Basque's men don't go in for Russian military haircuts. But it's best to assume that all the bad guys are out there."

"Waiting isn't doing us any good," Takigawa says.

"No, let's get this done."

"Do you want your rifles?" Heth asks.

"No, it's going to be tight in there. Hand me one of those bottles."

Heth hands me one of the IEDs and I zip it into the leather case on my belt. Takigawa and I draw our Mark 23s, press-check the chambers.

Most people consider pistols to be defensive weapons.

The Mark 23 was designed for use by operators as an *offensive* handgun. In extreme close quarters, a pistol can be superior to a submachine gun or short-barreled M4.

"We're going to work," I tell Heth. "If you see anyone approach, phone me. My phone is on vibrate, so I *will* feel it. I may or may not pick up. If I do, communicate quickly and clearly. How many, where, how armed."

Takigawa and I go the long way around. The sun is up. The fiery orb casts long shadows on the street. Makes it difficult to see. The contrast between glaring light and deep shadow is stark. The cobbled lanes and squares are filling with people. Tourists and locals. The locals are going about their business, or preparing for the day's festivities.

We walk straight to the front door of 25A. The pharmacy is still closed. I wouldn't be surprised if it stayed closed all day, or opened for business mid-afternoon. Takigawa steps to the right, I step to the left. Out of the corner of my eye, I see one of the two men in the Citroën lift a squad radio to his ear. If they're Leandro's, we'll receive a hot reception. I don't think so. They're Basque. Or Russian.

It's a wooden door, and the lock is a brass doorknob with a keyhole in the center. It must be fifty or sixty years old. I take the doorknob in my right hand and turn it both ways. It's locked.

Takigawa stands with his back to the door and faces the street. I brace myself, grip the knob, and pull hard. There's a splintering sound. The doorknob and cover plate separate from the old wood and come away in my hand. I take a multi-tool from my pocket. The interior knob is loose, and I poke it out. It falls to the floor on the other side with a clunk. I hold my breath, listen for the sound of people approaching from within. Nothing.

My multi-tool has a flat-head screwdriver. The lock's cylinder is loose. I insert the screwdriver head into a slot in the side of the cylinder. One twist, and the locking pins retract. The door swings open and we're greeted by the smell of moldy wood.

I step into the space behind the doorway. As expected, a long, narrow staircase leads to the second floor. I climb the stairs, setting my feet on the sides of each step, not the middle. I hold the Mark 23 at retracted high-ready. When I reach the landing, I step to one side of the inner front door. My left shoulder to the door, I hold the pistol in my right hand, support it with my left. I keep it close to my chest, pointing at the door. Center Axis Relock, a stance designed for extreme close quarters.

Takigawa follows me up the stairs. He mirrors my stance. Stands with his right shoulder to the door, pistol in his left hand.

The lock on this door is sturdy. I reach forward with my left hand and gently test the knob. It's locked. I nod to Takigawa. He pivots to his left, away from the door. Bends at the waist and mule-kicks it.

The door jamb splinters. I burst in, dig the left corner. Takigawa follows me, nut-to-butt. Digs the right corner. The first room, a sitting room, is empty. The kitchen is empty. There's a window and a door that opens to the fire escape. The window is shuttered and barred. There are three locks on the fire escape door. To the left of the kitchen is a door that leads to the bedroom.

I step forward, advance to the bedroom. Takigawa follows me. The interior door is ajar and I push it open. Step inside, dig left. Takigawa follows an inch behind, digs right. The bedroom is empty.

There is a single bed in the center of the tiny room. A threadbare white bedspread covers the bed and its two pillows.

On the exact geometric center of the bed lies a black mobile phone.

30

SEVILLE – SATURDAY, MORNING

L eandro's burner. It's a joke. He left it here, expecting us to track it. I pick it up, look at Takigawa, shake my head.

"We knew this was coming," Takigawa says.

My phone buzzes. It's Heth. I hit the send key.

"What's up?"

"One man on the way. Front steps. I can't see a weapon."

"Thanks."

I disconnect the call. Hold up one finger to Takigawa, go back into the living room. We stand on either side of the door and level our weapons.

There's a footstep on the landing.

"Breed, I am coming in. Don't shoot."

Orlov pushes the front door open, displays his hands, steps into the room.

"Orlov, what are you, the proverbial bad penny?"

"What a quaint expression. May I lower my hands?"

"Go ahead."

"I suspect by now you know who your young ward is."

"Yes."

"The princess is the legitimate ruler of Marethia. Tibor Szabo, the regent, is safe in Hungary. His role is to manage the transition to her rule. The prime minister and his people are usurpers. My task is to convey the princess to the regent so she can assume her rightful place on the throne."

"What do you want, Orlov?"

The colonel clasps his hands behind his back. "I should think that's obvious."

"Spell it out for me."

"I want to join forces. Did Anya Stein send you to Arles on purpose? I don't think so, but it does not matter. Your actions since that first night in Rodilhan indicate that your motives are pure. We are *both* on the right side of history."

"How did you track her to Rodilhan?"

"I tracked her to Arles, just as the usurpers did. Our intelligence services learned the usurpers hired The Basque to kill her. I decided to track The Basque. Sure enough, The Basque kidnapped a charming young man operating at the railroad station. They took him to a garage and extracted information from him. It was messy and noisy. The kind of thing we have both seen Islamic women do to prisoners."

The colonel smiles. "Yes, Breed. I know that story about you. More important, I know it is true."

I shot Afghan women who were flaying captured American soldiers alive. To spare the Army embarrassment, I allowed myself to be honorably discharged.

"The Basque was more creative," Orlov says. "His men flayed the boy with a deboning knife. When they finished, they lowered him naked into a vat of salt water."

I feel like I'm about to lose my breakfast. Wait. I haven't had breakfast.

Orlov smiles. "I suppose the Afghan women didn't have access to a metal plating facility like The Basque did. The boy told The Basque everything he knew, and more. I am certain he invented stories. The point is, The Basque learned it was Leandro Gabarri who took the girl. And he learned where she was being held."

"How did *you* learn this?"

"You and I use the same tactics, techniques and procedures. The TTP we jealously keep from the uninitiated. My ears are still ringing from the boy's screams. The Basque could have dissolved the boy's carcass in a vat of acid. No, he left it in a dumpster behind the train station."

"Sorry, Orlov. I'm going to recover the girl without your help."

"Then what, Breed? Will you allow her to fulfill her destiny?"

I haven't thought that far ahead.

My phone vibrates in my pocket. It's Heth.

"What's up?"

"Four men climbing the stairs. Shotguns and submachine guns. Four men climbing the fire escape. Shotguns and submachine guns."

"There are men outside," I say to Orlov. "Yours?"

"Negative."

"Stay where you are," I tell Heth. "Keep the engine running."

Z84s raised, two men burst through the front door. Orlov grabs the muzzle of the first man's gun and chops him across the throat. The man chokes and his knees give way. Orlov draws a Browning Hi-Power 9mm pistol. Shoots the man twice in the back of the head.

From retention, I fire my Mark 23. Double action, long

first pull. Two in the chest, one in the face. The second man
pitches onto his back. I unzip the leather pouch at my hip,
step to the doorway, and lob the perfume bottle down the
stairs.

There's a dull thump. Like a massive lung, the house
sucks a breath. The floorboards rise and jolt us off our feet.
The living room wall adjacent to the staircase bows inward.
A cloud of dust and smoke billows through the front door
and blows it off its hinges. Dust falls from the ceiling and
drifts in the air. The concussion squeezes my guts and blurs
my vision.

Two shotgun blasts, seconds apart. There's a crash and
two men kick the fire escape door off its hinges. Prone on the
floor, Takigawa and Orlov blaze away with their pistols. The
intruders jerk like puppets.

I go to the front door and look down the stairs.

There are *no* front stairs. The IED blew all the risers to
matchwood. Knocked the outer door off its hinges. There's
nothing left of the staircase but a gaping chasm. Nothing left
of the two men who were climbing the stairs. No one's
coming that way now.

My phone buzzes against my thigh.

It's Heth, warning me. More men are storming the fire
escape. I hurdle Orlov and Takigawa, dash to the fire escape
door. I get there in time to run into a man as he reaches the
landing. With the Mark 23, I muzzle thump him in the
throat. He drops his weapon and his eyes bug. I shoot him in
the face and he topples back against his partner.

Behind them, a big man with a beard. Armand Le Cagot
—The Basque.

The two men in the lead tumble down the fire escape
stairs and fall against The Basque. One man dead, the other

falling, trying to bring his weapon to bear. I charge down the stairs, point-shoot the second man in the face.

A bullet snaps past my ear. The Basque has caught the falling bodies, braced himself against their weight. He uses them for cover. Points the Beretta at me and fires again and again.

The Basque has cover, I don't. I hurl myself down the stairs and land on top of the two bodies. He can't support all three of us. We roll down the stairs in a furball. Land on the pavement.

The Basque and I struggle to free ourselves from the tangle. Lying on my back, I see Orlov and Takigawa at the top of the fire stairs. The Basque sees them too, realizes he's outnumbered. He scrambles to his feet and runs.

Sirens wail. The streets are filling with people, it'll take the cops an hour to get here. The Basque barges through the crowd. Turns and draws down on me. I dive into a doorway as he fires. He misses, hits a tourist center mass, right in the chest. The middle-aged woman goes down hard. Her husband, in Bermuda shorts and a straw hat, falls to his knees next to her and shouts for help.

A Spanish policeman runs toward us from the other direction. Maybe police vehicles can't get through, but there must be foot patrols in the area.

The Basque and the policeman see each other at the same time. The cop reaches for his sidearm. The Basque shoots him before he can clear his holster. The policeman goes down. The Basque turns on me, pistol raised in a Weaver grip.

Passers-by have run or thrown themselves to the ground. I have a clear shot. I fire twice. One round hits The Basque in his weapon, the other catches him in the throat. He drops the Beretta and lifts his hands. Blood squirts between his fingers. He tries to run while holding his hands over the wound.

I pound two more rounds into his back, between the shoulder blades. The Basque pitches forward onto his face. Weapon raised, I approach from behind. He's not moving, but I take no chances. I put another round in the back of his head.

Decock the Mark 23, conceal it under my shirt. The shooting's done. It was over so quickly, most people haven't a clue what happened. The woman who got shot is dead. Her husband is kneeling next to her, sobbing. Once again, people fill the street. They still have places to go and things to do. This shooting will be a minor incident in the story of their lives.

I turn into a narrow alley, approach the pickup from the rear. Heth is behind the wheel, Takigawa in the front seat. I jerk open the rear passenger door and get in. "Let's go," I say. "Back out and head the other way."

Heth throws the pickup in reverse. Left hand at twelve o'clock, she twists around in her seat so she can look over her shoulder. She drives backwards, pushing pedestrians aside as she goes. When she reaches the intersection, she spins the wheel to leave the lane and turn into the wider street. She shifts into drive and heads west in the direction of the *Maestranza*.

Right into a mess of tiny streets and lanes.

"Where's Orlov?" I ask.

"When you took off, we went down the fire stairs together. I went straight back to the truck, he got into that Citroën with the two guys in it. They drove off, totally chill."

"Anybody pay attention to this truck?"

Takigawa shakes his head. "No one noticed the gunfight on the fire escape, no one noticed the shooting on the second floor. The explosion on the stairs blew the door off, they'll call the fire department. It'll take them an hour to get here."

"Those sirens?"

"Until The Basque shot the cop, I would have said fire department. Now I think the cops are on their way too."

I let out a breath, lean back in my seat. Take the bag with the last three IEDs and tuck it between my feet. "Get back on the highway. We need to meet Stein at Morón."

"I've never seen thirty million Euros."

"You know, there was one other person watching what happened back there."

"The Gypsy King, right?"

I take Leandro's burner from my pocket. "Yes. He left this for us."

31

MORÓN – SATURDAY, EARLY AFTERNOON

S tein steps through the Morón Air Base front gate and strides to us. The CIA's Deputy Director of Special Situations never changes. Slim, thirtyish, conservatively dressed in tailored clothes. Her shoulder length dark hair has been tied back. She wears her signature black pants suit and flat, sensible dress shoes.

She's carrying a black nylon duffel bag slung over her right shoulder. It's a cylinder three feet long and a foot in diameter. It looks heavy. Over her left shoulder she carries her signature black leather briefcase. It's the perfect size for her laptop.

I get out of the air-conditioned pickup to help her. "Let me take that for you."

Stein unslings the duffel and sets it down between us. She isn't sweating. Her black suit is a kind of ultra-light linen. It must feel like she's wearing nothing thicker than a T-shirt.

"Breed, you can't stay out of trouble, can you?" Stein smiles from behind her dark sunglasses. "I send you on vacation and you get into a shooting war your very first day."

"Orlov thinks you might have sent me to Arles on purpose."

"I'm flattered, but I'm not *that* devious."

I'm not so sure. "Is that what thirty million Euros looks like?"

"Take a look."

I push the bag onto its side and open it. Look inside, zip it shut.

"Are you up for this?" Stein asks.

"Always. Are you?"

"What do *you* think?"

Stein's always been a field operator. She took the riskiest jobs—gambles that boosted her career. The SIG P226 Legion she carries under her suit jacket is there to be used.

I carry the ransom to the front passenger door. Takigawa gets out and we load it between passenger and driver. We already have the rifles and ammunition on the floor of the passenger cab. Along with three IEDs we need to keep safe and cool.

Stein slides onto the passenger bench next to Heth. The girl is *not* happy. She gives me a dirty look that says, *You told me she wasn't coming.*

"See that bag between Heth's feet?" I ask Stein.

"Yes."

"Whatever happens, don't step on it, don't drop it, don't drop anything on it."

"What is it, a doomsday device?"

"Good guess. It's three very sensitive IEDs, any one of which could convert this pickup into a smoking hole in the ground."

"For God's sake, Breed. Where did you get them?"

"I made them. All us little boys blew up their dad's garage when we were kids."

I've left the engine and air conditioning running to keep the IEDs cool. Get in behind the wheel, shift into drive, and head back toward Seville.

"Have you heard from the Gypsy King?" Stein asks.

"No, but he won't be long."

"How do you know?"

I tell Stein what happened in the *barrio*. "He knew we'd geolocate his phone. Left it for us like an inside joke. I'm sure he'll call to collect his money."

Stein frowns. "The French police have you and Rincón on a list."

"Did they find the bodies?"

"It took them a week to miss the sixth-floor laundry. Cleaning ladies noticed a smell in the linen closet. Forensics had a hard time working out the time of death, so they are questioning all guests who occupied the sixth floor last week."

"I'll tell them I heard nothing. Slept like a baby."

"The deaths match your MO. One man killed by a blow from behind. Broke his neck. The second guy was disabled hand-to-hand, then took two in the face."

"The world is so violent these days."

"Another two men were found dead in a small suburb of Valencia. A place called Cheste."

"I'm innocent."

"I bet."

"*Orlov* killed them."

"I wonder if he drives *his* people crazy."

"Their highest authority hung the Order of St George around his neck."

"I don't expect any blowback," Stein says. "I just want you to know that you are leaving footprints."

"We're going to leave a few more."

The burner in my pocket rings. I usually set my phones to vibrate. Leandro's burner plays an energetic flamenco tune that blends Spanish guitar, tap and castanets. I want that ringtone—for my vacation playlist.

"Do you have the money, Breed?"

I'll say this for Leandro. He comes right to the point.

"Yes."

"Good. Find a comfortable place in Santa Cruz. Have dinner, go dancing. We will meet in the *Maestranza*. I will call with instructions. Make certain you are close enough to arrive quickly."

"Where's the girl?"

"The girl is alive. If anything goes wrong, if we smell police, she dies."

"Let me speak with her."

"All in good time, Breed."

Leandro disconnects the call.

"What does he want?" Stein asks.

"He wants to meet at the *Maestranza*. He'll call to tell us when and how."

"Why would he tell us where?"

"He wants to make sure we can get to the *Maestranza* quickly. Tomorrow is Resurrection Sunday, the last day of Semana Santa. Tonight, the streets will be packed with processions and celebrants."

32

SEVILLE – SATURDAY, EARLY EVENING

Magellan Navigator displays a 3D rendering of the *Maestranza*, the great Seville bullring. It's not the largest bullring in Spain, but it is the oldest. And Seville is the heart of bullfighting.

"We have to put ourselves in Leandro's shoes," I say. "Consider how he'll arrange the exchange."

I sit in the center of an alcove in a dark bar, manipulating the image on Stein's laptop. She sits on my right, and we've tucked the sack of money on the floor between my right leg and her left. Takigawa sits next to me, and Heth sits on the other side of Stein. The bag of IEDs is nestled between Heth's feet. The seat curves around the recessed table, and we huddle to view the image.

A male singer bursts into a flamenco song. The melody and his voice wrench one's heart. The Spanish are a dark and passionate race. The French enjoy a certain *bon vivre*, the Italians, *la dolce vita*. The Spanish soul is soaked in tragedy. There are no happy fucking endings.

Will this be a Spanish story?

I look across the table at Heth. "I tried to keep you out of this."

"Not very hard."

"Losing Ballard cost us. I need you on the long rifle."

"I told you before—I didn't come here to kill people."

The image of Julia, naked at Leandro's feet, makes me quiver with rage. "These people *need* killing."

Silent, Heth stares at me.

I hold my breath.

"Breed, only for *you*. Understand?"

That's a Salish Indian talking. They say what they mean and mean what they say. I allow myself to absorb Heth's words. "Thank you."

"That's where I need to be." Heth has accepted her role. All business, she points to an imposing balcony. Framed by Doric columns, it's high on the shady side of the ring, set on the second level of the bleachers.

The structure is the *palco principe*, the balcony reserved for the royal family. To the left and right of the royal balcony are *palcos* for the bullring's president and VIPs. Fronted by an ornate balustrade, it provides a grand view of the events.

"No," I tell her. "You need to be on the other side."

"Why?" Heth looks doubtful. "That balcony is best for overwatch."

"That," Takigawa says, "is why the Gypsy King's men will occupy it. They picked the location. They'll arrive before us."

"There's another balcony under the clock." I look across the table at Heth. "From there, you'll have a clear shot at their sniper."

"Why won't *he* be under the clock?"

"For their purposes, it's on the wrong side of the *Maes-tranza*. The royal balcony sits directly above the *puerta prin-*

cipe. That gate opens onto the river highway—their quickest route out of the city."

"They'll control how we enter," Takigawa says. "Direct our movement through pre-arranged fields of fire."

"Look at the gates," I say. "There are six gates at ground level. If we take the royal balcony as twelve o'clock, they are located at two, four, six, eight, and ten. Four of them are important to the spectacle. Clockwise from the top, they are the *puerta principe*—through which the champion matador departs on the shoulders of fans. The *puerta de arrastre* is at two o'clock—it's the dragging gate through which they haul out dead bulls. At four is the *puerta de toriles*, from which the bull enters the ring. At six is the *puerta de cuadrillas*. From there, the parade of matadors enters at the start of the event. It's also the gate through which the picadors and horses enter and leave."

"It's not a circle," Stein says. "It's a blob."

"You're so *analytical*." I enjoy teasing Stein. "It's an irregular ellipse, but close enough. *Other* bullrings are circular."

Stein gives me a dirty look. "You study up for this?"

"I research my vacations. I wanted to learn about bull-fighting."

Heth scowls. "So what do we do?"

"If I'm right, they'll have us bring the money through the *puerta de cuadrillas*. That allows them to enter through one or more of the gates close to the river. Probably the *puerta de arrastre*. They'll post a sniper on the royal balcony. The bullring's field is called the *ruedo*. I think they'll want to do the exchange in the middle."

"You're not going out there," Heth says.

"I don't think I'll have a choice. The Gypsy King will have to bring Julia out. All three of us will be on the X."

Heth leans across the table and squints at the dynamic scale at the bottom of the image. She takes a white paper napkin and a ballpoint pen. I tilt the screen to give her a better view. Heth lays the napkin over the image, marks various distances on the paper in black ink. Satisfied, she leans back in her seat, fusses with the napkin. Folds it repeatedly, unfolds it.

"The *ruedo* is sixty yards across," Heth says. "From the bleachers at six o'clock to the president's balcony is a hundred yards. Fifty to the center of the ring."

Those are police sniper distances. Military snipers often work between a hundred and eight hundred yards. Police and military Squad Designated Marksmen usually engage at closer ranges. That doesn't make the job easier. Police have to contend with civilians in the kill zone.

"You know your holdovers." Heth doesn't need a lecture on marksmanship. "When we enter the structure, you have to make your way upstairs to the second level. Carry a sidearm, sling your rifle until you get to the top."

"Why?"

"I reckon the Gypsy King has four or five men. He doesn't know we're going to have overwatch, but you might run into one up there."

"If they're controlling our approach, they'll have someone watching for us," Takigawa says.

"Yes. One man with a phone. He'll watch us enter. Follow us, come from behind. You have to pull rear security, take him out."

"They'll kill the girl," Stein says.

"Not if we're quiet about it. Once we're inside, Takigawa will ambush him. Once our shadow is gone, Heth will be free to climb. There are interior stairs leading right to the top. It's like any stadium. The second level has vendors on a circular concourse. Like spokes on a wheel, alleys lead to the bleachers."

"What are these platforms under the floodlights?" Heth asks. "They're high ground, above the balconies."

"Service platforms," I tell her. "I don't want you there, because there's no cover and concealment."

"*Puerta de cuadrillas* is a funnel," Takigawa says.

"That's why they'll want us to come through it. They know I'll bring backup. They, on the other hand, arrive first and have a choice of gates to get onto the *ruedo*. Before we get to the gate, Heth will be on overwatch. I want *you* to climb to the second level on the left. Find a way onto the bleachers. Stein, you come with me. Remember, if shooting starts, you can conceal yourself behind the *barrera*, that brown fence that goes clear around the ring. Remember the coliseum walls are stone, but the fence is wood. It won't stop bullets."

"It's a shooting gallery," Stein says.

"Yes, a two-way shooting gallery."

"Will you carry the IEDs into the ring?" Heth asks.

"No. I reckon we'll be working over ranges that are too great to throw them."

"This venue is great for the Gypsy King," Takigawa says. "The *puerta principe* is right next to the river and main roads. After the exchange, they leave that way. Breed, flip the image so we're looking straight down."

I click on a button and Magellan switches to a bird's-eye view of the *Maestranza*.

"I'm guessing those open spaces flush to the back wall are pens," Takigawa says.

"The *coralles* are adjacent to the *puerta de toriles*." I flick the cursor over the concrete structures. "No roofs, so you can look down at the bulls from a catwalk above. The bulls are led straight from the pens into the arena. Further along the ring, near the *puerta de cuadrillas*, are the *cuadras caballos*, the horse stables."

The *Maestranza* backs onto a curved alley. On the other side of the alley is a street of apartment buildings and *bodegas*. The warehouses have long been converted into offices. They are not the priciest addresses in town. Their view of the Guadalquivir is blocked by the massive white stone face of the *Maestranza* . The alley is so narrow, it never sees the light of day.

"The animals must be brought in that way," Takigawa says.

"Yes. The streets will be packed tomorrow, so the animals were brought in this afternoon."

Takigawa jerks his chin at the screen. "Let's look at the interior."

I manipulate the cursor and the arrow keys. Drop to the level of the *ruedo* and try to push through the dragging gate. The screen dissolves into a mass of jumbled lines. When the image resolves, we're back in the alley outside the pens.

"Magellan has no data for the interior," I tell him. "It works from photographs and satellite imagery."

"Maybe photography isn't allowed inside."

"Under the stands, the bullring is vast. You can get lost in there. We'll have to play it by ear."

I reach for my beer.

"What do we do now?" Heth asks.

"Now, we wait," I tell her.

We don't have to wait long. I let Heth and the others take turns manipulating the Magellan rendition of the *Maes-*

tranza. Finish my beer, watch the flamenco dancers, listen to the music. When the phone rings, I know it will be Leandro.

I thumb the send button. "Breed."

"Come to the *Maestranza* at midnight," Leandro says.

"The gate behind the *cuadras caballos* will be unlocked. Bring the money to the *puerta de cuadrillas* and wait at the *barrera*. I will telephone you there."

"I want to see the girl."

"You will. Remember, I will have a rifle on her. If anything goes wrong, she dies."

Leandro disconnects the call. I pocket the phone and look around the table.

"He's playing it exactly as we expected," I say.

"*High Noon* at the bullring?" Takigawa smiles.

"No, midnight. Let's go."

33

LA MAESTRANZA – EASTER SUNDAY, EARLY MORNING

The *Maestranza* glowers at us from across the river highway. We decided to leave the pickup at the bar and take a taxi to the ring. I pay the driver, and Takigawa hauls our luggage out of the trunk. The black nylon bag of money and two olive drab duffels. Heth's AR-15 and Takigawa's M4.

It's dark, and the white walls of the bullring shine in the street lamps. The front of the bullring is mobbed with processions of penitents and floats. The various orders shuffle north, some pulling their floats on carts, others bearing the weight on their shoulders. The penitents wear their long colored cloaks and pointy hoods. Black, white, crimson, blue, and violet. They come in all manner of combinations.

I stare at the malevolent bulk of the *Maestranza*. This is why I came to Seville. Months ago, I planned my vacation. I was determined to visit the historical bullring before bull-fighting was banned altogether.

Why? Because the *Maestranza* stinks of death. For three hundred years, its golden sand has been watered with blood. Thousands of bulls, of course. Horses, too. Brutally gored before the introduction of body armor in 1928. And men. Bullfighters like Rincón, drawn to display their courage and skill for fame and fortune. Sometimes wanting, often unlucky. The sand is carefully raked over before the start of the next fight. The blood is covered, added to the spoor of centuries.

Tonight a different contest will take place. For the life of Princess Julia of Marethia.

We stand in line abreast. I take a breath and step forward, march toward the *puerta principe*. When we reach the procession, I push my way through the river of penitents, ignore their protests.

When we reach the big gate, I look left toward the museum. The alley is tight, but there are not as many people in the alley as there are on the street outside. I look right. There is a smaller door with *Administracion* printed in white letters on its face. The alley to the right is as narrow as that to the left. It runs the entire circumference of the *Maestranza*.

I reach under my jacket, lay my hand on the butt of the Mark 23. Turn right, enter the alley. First Stein, then Heth, follow me. Takigawa brings up the rear.

This alley leads to the business end of the bullring. The path to the left leads to the museum and the areas open to tourists. I wanted to see the real *Maestranza*, the bullring that tourists don't see. In my wildest imagination, I never thought I would visit it like this.

Slow is fast. I walk down the alley, hand on my pistol. My eyes search the shadows left and right. Bullring gates on the left, doorways to the renovated houses and *bodegas* on the right. We've been told to enter through a ticket gate at the back, near the *cuadras caballos*. The sun sets in the west, behind the royal balcony. The president and VIPs sit in the *sobre*, the shady part of the ring. The bullfighters, the animals, and poor people enter via the east gates. That's the *sol* side, the seats that bake in the merciless sun.

I pass the gates at the ten o'clock, then those at the eight. I sweep the alley in front of me, then the overhead. I know Takigawa will be doing the same.

The hot, earthy smell of horse manure drifts from the stables. Behind me, Stein chokes. The boxes and expensive seats are far away on the other side. The crowds pay for the death and gore of the bullfight. The smell of horseshit is too much reality.

We've passed the tiny chapel reserved for bullfighters. The royal chapel, viewed by tourists through a set of barred gates, is on the northwest side, diametrically opposite us.

My eyes search the gloom. Close to the seven o'clock stands a metal gate. This is the one we've been told to use. I raise my right fist, signal the others to stop.

The gate is constructed of tall, vertical lengths of lead pipe, cross-braced at five-foot intervals. The lattice between the pipes is rough chicken wire. Chest high, a chain hangs from one of the cross-braces. It was used to secure the gate with a heavy padlock. Open, the lock dangles from the chain.

We're expected.

I open the gate, wince at the sharp squeak, and step inside. This gate is tall so that horses can enter. They are then led to the stables on the left. To the right is a brown wooden door with iron hinges painted black. Gently, I pull it open.

The interior is lit by dim, 25-watt bulbs. I step to the right and follow the border of the bullring's inner wall until I come to a wide arcade. To the left is a long alley that leads to the *puerta de cuadrillas*. I turn into it and strain my ears to hear the others behind me.

I glance back. Stein and Heth are there. Heth is carrying two duffels. Hers and Takigawa's. The Delta sniper is nowhere to be seen. He's concealed himself in the shadows, waiting for the gypsy who must be following us. I step to the wall of the alley and strain my ears. Stein and Heth do the same.

From the arcade behind comes a barely audible thump. Takigawa's suppressed Mark 23 pistol. He used the weapon's slide lock to prevent the action from cycling.

Takigawa's form emerges from the gloom. He meets my eyes, raises his left thumb. Takes his duffel from Heth. Our gypsy shadow has been eliminated.

Without a word, Heth and Takigawa take out their weapons. Takigawa dons a load-bearing vest. The vest has six magazines velcroed to the front in two vertical columns. Heth slings the long-barreled AR-15 and Steiner variable-power optic across her back. She squeezes a spare magazine into her hip pocket and draws the BM from her waistband. Takigawa and Heth leave the empty duffels on the floor and kick them to one side.

I watch them go back into the arcade. Heth goes left and Takigawa right. They're making for the interior stairs that will take them to the second level. I check my watch. They have five minutes to reach their positions.

Stein draws her SIG. Meets my eyes in the dark.

I lead her down the alley. It's wide and high-ceilinged.

High enough to accommodate picadors on horseback.

Ahead of us stands the *puerta de cuadrillas*.

Princess Julia waits on the other side.

With her consort, whose name is Death.

34

LA MAESTRANZA – EASTER SUNDAY, EARLY MORNING

I take a deep breath and push open the wide gate. It swings aside on oiled hinges. Beyond the *barrera* lies the vast expanse of the *ruedo*, the majestic sweep of the *Maestranza*. The bullring's structure is dark against a night sky lit by fireworks. Outside the bullring's walls, I hear the rattle of firecrackers.

My phone rings. I push the send button and hold it to my ear. It's Leandro.

"Walk to the center of the ring, Breed. Bring the money."

The Gypsy King's voice is calm and deliberate.

"Bring out the girl."

Floodlights blaze and the *ruedo* is bathed in brilliant white light.

I motion Stein to hang back in the shadows. Step past the *barrera*.

The *puerta de arrastre* swings open. Two horses with riders advance. Hands bound behind her back, a thin figure sits on one of the horses. The figure's head and shoulders have been shrouded with a penitent's pointy black hood.

The figure has Julia's build, but all I see are her eyes, visible through holes cut in the cloth.

On the ground, Leandro walks with a phone to his ear.

"I know you brought a man and two women," Leandro says. "It doesn't matter. I have a rifle on the girl, and Jaime has a shotgun pointed at her head. If you try anything, we will kill her. The rifle will remain on her for half an hour after we leave. If you or your people try anything, if the police stop us outside, if anyone tries to follow us, you will carry home a corpse without a head."

Leandro disconnects the call and we pocket our phones.

With measured steps, we advance. I imagine gunfighters stalking each other, or a cold war exchange of prisoners at Checkpoint Charlie.

The man called Jaime rides on the girl's right. He carries a double-barreled shotgun in his right hand, pointed at the girl's head. The reins of the girl's horse are held loosely in his left. Leandro walks on the other side.

We meet in the center of the *ruedo*, six feet apart.

Leandro's sniper will be on the *palco principe*. If not between the Doric columns, in the president's box, his rifle trained on me. Resting on a rolled-up jacket laid over the front rail. One twitch and my lights will go out before I'm aware he's fired.

I didn't expect Jaime and his shotgun.

Who will Heth go after first—Jaime or the sniper? Her mission is to protect Julia. At a range of three feet, Jaime is the greater threat. I would shoot him first, but I don't know what Heth will do. One target is fifty yards away, the other a hundred. She will have to adjust her holdover on the fly.

The air is close. Thank goodness for small favors—there's no wind.

"Show us the money, Breed."

"Show me the girl."

The gypsy snorts. "Jaime."

The man on the horse holds the shotgun steady with his right hand. He reaches over with his left and jerks the black hood from the girl's head.

Floodlit, Julia's blond hair shines like gold. Her face is drawn and white. Pleading, her eyes meet mine.

I slip the nylon duffel from my shoulder. With a grunt, I throw it onto the ground at Leandro's feet. The bag hits the ground with a thud. My mouth tastes like sand. "*You* open it."

Leandro is wearing black jeans, a blue work shirt, and a maroon *chaleco*, embroidered with gold thread. He carries his Beretta Cheetah stuffed into his waistband. It wouldn't be my choice, but he prefers the ivory-handled knife sheathed at his hip.

With cold eyes, the gypsy appraises me. Bends to one knee and unzips the duffel. I watch the zipper slide, and the bag's nylon folds split open like the lips of a wound. Shredded paper spills onto the sand.

The gypsy freezes. Stares at me.

"Listen." My voice is soft, barely above a whisper. "I have a rifle on *you*. Close the bag, pick it up, and walk away. If you don't, *my* man will kill you. Walk away and we *all* live."

Blood roars in my ears. I have no idea how the man will react.

Leandro's eyes burn and now I know he'll go crazy. The gypsy turns and sprints for the open gate. "Kill the girl!"

Jaime's head explodes. A halo of blood and bits of tissue glitters in the floodlights. The image is frozen in my brain for an instant. Then he crumples and falls from his horse. The crack of Heth's rifle echoes in the *Maestranza*.

I grab Julia by the arm and the front of her shirt. With one motion, I jerk her from the horse and throw her to the ground. There's another shot and the horse bucks, then drops. Leandro's sniper missed Julia, hit her mount in the back. Jaime's horse bolts. I throw myself flat on top of Julia as the sniper fires again.

A white-hot knife slashes my left thigh. I spread myself over Julia like a blanket. Try to cover every part of her with every part of *me*. Cheek-to-cheek, our faces touch as I try to cover her head with mine. Her blue eyes are stoned with fear. My eyes slide toward the great clock. Heth fires a second time. From the clock balcony, a muzzle flash stabs the night.

Behind us, a man cries out.

I wait for a bullet to slam into me. Nothing. Heth must have hit the sniper.

Chaos erupts. Rifle fire crackles from the north and south bleachers. Pistol fire echoes from the *puerta de cuadrillas*. I roll over, drag Julia to the wounded horse. The animal lies on its side, kicking. I shove her against its back and lie next to her. Reach down and untie her hands. She's been bound with three-eighths inch twisted hemp. The cruel jute fibers have scraped her wrists bloody.

Bullets whack into the wounded horse. It jerks with the impact. It's alive, I can feel its chest heaving as it struggles to breathe. Its sweat stinks of terror. Bullets shred the duffel bag and scatter paper across the *ruedo*. I draw my Mark 23 and fire at the flashes twinkling on the north bleachers.

Stein and Takigawa lay down cover fire. Takigawa alternates fire between the two men. Stein focuses on the man to the north.

"Are you alright?" I ask Julia.

"Yes. Are you?"

"I've been hit."

"Give me that."

Julia takes the rope. Twists on her side, back to the horse, front to me. She reaches down, fashions a tourniquet around my thigh, and cinches it tight.

More bullets stitch the wounded horse. The animal's nostrils flare and it groans. Blood and spit pour from its mouth. It can barely lift its head. I hold Julia next to the dying animal. Crush her against it with my body.

Stein dashes toward us from the gate. Arm extended, she fires at the north bleachers. The scene in the bullring is surreal. Jaime's horse, panicked, gallops this way and that. The animal darts from one end of the *ruedo* to the other. Desperate to escape, it tries to jump out of the ring. It clatters against the wooden planks, bounces off the *barrera*.

The bleachers afford no cover. Takigawa and the gypsies stand in the openings of the concrete tunnels that lead to the interior concourse. The gypsy to the north alternates fire between us and Takigawa.

Stein throws herself down next to me. She drops a mag, pulls another from her hip pocket. "Loading," she says.

I turn onto my side, fire at the north bleachers. Stein slaps a fresh magazine into her SIG, resumes fire. The rifleman is firing in short bursts. One burst at us, another at Takigawa. A bullet hits Takigawa in the chest and he pitches backward into the tunnel.

The gypsy on the south balcony steps from cover. He moves on Takigawa, firing his rifle. I brace my forearms on the flanks of the horse and empty the Mark 23 at him. The gunman retreats behind the concrete wall of the tunnel. Still in the fight, Takigawa struggles to his feet.

Another crack echoes from the clock balcony. The gypsy to the north crumples.

I drop my empty, slap a fresh magazine into the Mark 23.

"Watch her," I tell Stein.

Get up, run toward the *puerta de arrastre*. At the first stride, pain sears my wounded leg and it buckles. I pitch forward and eat sand. There's a flash from the black maw of the tunnel, and a bullet snaps over my head. I fire one-handed, lurch to my feet. There's an answering shot and another miss. Limping, I press on.

The Gypsy King fires again. Heth fires over my head, covering me. Leandro retreats into the *puerta*.

Leandro's got the Cheetah, but he's a lousy shot. With a handgun, in this light, it's hard to hit a moving target.

I advance as quickly as my wounded leg allows. Heth continues to fire over my head. Leandro fires again and again. The sound of his .380 is distinctive. *Pop, pop, pop.* Heth doesn't have a night scope, but the gypsy's muzzle flashes are something to aim at. There are seven rounds in that gun, eight if he keeps one in the chamber. He's spent six.

When we're separated by ten yards, I raise my pistol. Leandro and Heth stop shooting and I stumble past the *barrera*. Push through the gate.

The Gypsy King is gone.

35

LA MAESTRANZA – EASTER SUNDAY, EARLY MORNING

L eandro has disappeared inside the *Maestranza*. He's going to try to lose me in the warren of chambers beneath the stands.

Heth and Stein have pinned down the gunman in the south bleachers. Plain and simple, a sniper is an area control weapon. Heth can kill anything that moves over the bleachers and *ruedo*. Takigawa has disappeared down the tunnel. He's gone into the concourse, maneuvering to outflank Leandro's last gunman.

Focus. I carry the Mark 23 at retracted high ready, push into the tunnel beyond the *puerta de arrastre*. Like the *puerta de cuadrillas*, it's high-ceilinged. Riders on horses drag the carcasses of slain bulls down this tunnel. Take them to the *desolladero*, where they are butchered. The meat is loaded onto trucks and carried away. Again, I'm reminded that the *Maestranza*, an entertainment venue, reeks of death.

A loud pop carries from the corridor at the end of the tunnel. Glass tinkles on the floor and the corridor goes dark. I drag myself to the end of the tunnel. It's no different to

entering a room—it's about angles. I step to the right wall,
check the corridor to the left. Dim bulbs illuminate the clut-
ter. The passage stretches west to the *capilla real*, the royal
chapel. Beyond that, the *puerta principe* and the river
entrance. That's the natural exit for a man bent on getting
away. Step to the left wall, check the corridor to the right. It's
dark. The corridor follows the curve of the wall, and leads
north-by-east. Bricks in the distance are covered with layer
upon layer of greasy paint. Shiny in the light. There's
another pop, another tinkle of glass, and the light goes out.

Leandro is moving through the corridor, smashing light
bulbs as he goes, leaving me in darkness. He's heading
toward the back of the arena, the bay where the carcasses are
removed. There's only one reason for him not to take the
easy way out.

The Gypsy King wants to kill me before he escapes.

I follow him down the corridor. Wish I had night vision.
I'm clinging to the inviting glow, thirty feet further along.
The next bulb in a long series. Another pop and the glow
dissolves into darkness. I pass the *desolladero*. It's a small
slaughterhouse with an open gate that leads outside. There,
a skilled team de-horns, skins, and quarters the dead bulls.
Six bulls per *corrida*, fifteen minutes each. The meat is
carried away in trucks. Ahead, in the darkness, I smell
manure and wet straw. An ugly, nauseating assault on the
senses.

Animals shuffle and snort. The *coralles* are ahead, and
that means the bulls consigned for tomorrow's fight.
Another pop, and this time the interior goes completely
dark, except for the dimmest light that filters from the gate. I
freeze, wait for my night vision to adapt to the darkness.

Miura bulls are the most aggressive in the world. The best matadors, those secure in their reputations and income, avoid them. Only Rincón regularly accepts the challenge. My stomach hollows as I advance on the corral. Bulls together are calmer than bulls alone. Is that true of Miuras? I won't count on it.

Somewhere ahead, Leandro waits.

My eyes adjust to the gloom. Bulky shapes shuffle this way and that on cloven feet. Disturbed by their movement, straw rustles. Animals, each weighing three-quarters of a ton, grunt and snort. They are packed with mounds of muscle and sharp horns that can run a man through.

A Mark 23 can stop a charging bear. If I need it, the pistol can stop a charging bull. I hope it doesn't come to that.

With a loud, lowing groan, a massive head swings toward me. Startled, I jump back. Stand on my good leg, lean against the wall for support.

The crack of Leandro's pistol shot is deafening in the enclosed space. The muzzle flash lights the corral. I glimpse half a dozen animals. Mustache drooping, Leandro's mad face leers at me over open sights. Had the bull not startled me, the Gypsy King would have found his mark.

Darkness closes around us. The bulls, shocked by the gunshot, barge against each other. I sense a heavy object flying through the air. Twist to one side. Leandro's pistol strikes me a glancing blow on the side of the head. Clatters to the floor. Pain shoots through my temple like I've been pistol-whipped. The weapon was empty, the slide locked back. He threw the weapon at me.

In the darkness, the big gypsy launches himself across the corral. At extreme close quarters, in the black, I fire from retention. I manage one shot before he barrels into me. He slams into my midsection and the impact lifts me off my feet. He throws me against the wall and I drop the pistol.

He has me pinned. Grips my collar with his left hand, throws the hard edge of his forearm across my throat. Where's his right hand? Instinctively, I drop my left, block the thrust of his blade. Scream as the point penetrates my palm and comes out the other side.

In the blackness, red waves of pain wash over me. Leandro tries to jerk the knife loose, but I twist it to one side. The blade catches between the bones of my palm.

"*¡Bastardo!*" Leandro struggles to wrestle the blade free. I scream again. Blinded by the pain, I palm-strike his face with my free hand. Once, twice. That rings some bells. He lets go of the knife and topples sideways.

Neither of us can see. This is all kinesthesis. In the dark, we sense each other's location and orientation. He's on his knees, scrabbling on the floor with both hands. Desperately sweeping straw and excrement aside, searching for the gun.

I lash out with my foot. The toe of my shoe connects with something soft and Leandro grunts. My wounded leg gives out again. I crash against the wall and slide to the hard stone floor. Blood roars in my ears. With a cry, I jerk the knife from where it's buried in my palm. Lunge toward the gypsy. He's a black shape rising, extending the Mark 23.

A light stabs the darkness and pins Leandro's face in a brilliant oval frame. The gypsy's eyes widen with shock.

Crack. Like lightning, a muzzle flash sears the gloom and jolts my brain. A second shot follows the first and two black holes appear in the bridge of Leandro's nose. His head jerks and the Mark 23 falls from his hand. He collapses against the flank of a bull.

"Breed." It's Orlov. "Stay down."

The Russian colonel advances. He carries his Browning Hi-Power pistol in an isosceles, holds it on Leandro. When he is sure the gypsy is dead, he picks up the Mark 23.

"Can you stand?" Orlov asks.

"Yes." I get to my feet. Orlov continues to hold his pistol on Leandro. The flashlight mounted under the barrel casts dim illumination over the corral.

The bulls, mollified by the presence of their brothers, have shrunk to one side of the pen. They've formed a *querencia*, a space they will defend as their own. Provided we do not approach, we are safe from attack.

Leandro lies flat on his back, arms splayed. One leg is bent under the other. His dead eyes stare at the ceiling.

Orlov hands the Mark 23 to me. "I think we should see to our princess."

36

LA MAESTRANZA – EASTER SUNDAY, EARLY
MORNING

Orlov and I emerge from the *puerta de arrastre*. I've
torn a strip from my shirttail and bound the
wound in my hand. The blood is coagulating.
The Russian colonel saved my life, but I can't help looking at
him with suspicion.

Takigawa has joined Stein and Julia in the center of the
ruedo. Stein is examining his wound.

Julia looks up as Orlov and I approach. Throws herself at
me. The girl lays her face against my chest and hugs me
tight. Her cheeks are wet. Tension or genuine emotion. She
says nothing—the gesture says it all.

Heth approaches from the *puerta de cuadrillas*, her rifle
low ready.

I hold Julia close. She doesn't want to let go.

"You made the right choice," I tell Heth.

Heth accepts my thanks with a nod. "Had I gone for the
sniper, you couldn't have reached the other guy in time."

Gently, I separate myself from Julia. The girl steps back
and wipes her eyes.

Takigawa's bare chested. His wound is a nasty gash that extends from the side of his left pectoral muscle and passes under his armpit.

"It's just a graze," Stein says. She tears the sleeves off Takigawa's shirt and fashions a makeshift bandage. Hands him the shirt to wear as a vest.

I glance at the south bleachers. "Did you get him?" I ask.

"Dead as Kelsey's nuts," Takigawa says.

The night is filled with the rattle of firecrackers. High above the *Maestranza*, Roman candles explode in showers of flaming balls. The battle lasted ten minutes. The crowd dismissed the gunfire as part of the celebrations.

Orlov stares at the shredded duffel and the torn paper strewn across the *ruedo*. He turns to Stein. "You took quite a chance."

"I had no choice," Stein says. "We didn't have Princess Julia's family murdered, but I couldn't get approval to pay her ransom."

"Of course." Orlov's expression is grim. "Why save the last surviving member of the royal family, when their murderers are prepared to give you everything you want?"

"I don't make policy, Colonel." Stein brushes her hair back from her eyes. "We don't need the Palvet Pass. Weapons will continue to flow across the Polish border. And we can run them into Odessa from the Black Sea."

"One less route for us to interdict," Orlov says. "Very well, I will escort the princess to the regent. We will ensure that she assumes her rightful place on the throne."

"I don't think so, Colonel. The princess is under the protection of the United States."

Orlov squares himself in front of Stein. "*That* is unacceptable."

"We have you outnumbered, Colonel."

"Do you really think I came alone?"

My eyes flick to the *palco principe*. Have we been careless, or is the Russian bluffing?

"Enough," Julia says. She dabs her wet eyes with the back of her hand. "My duty is clear."

The sharp edge to the girl's tone shocks me. The five of us stare at her.

Julia straightens. "Colonel Orlov and Breed, together, shall escort me to Hungary."

"Princess Julia—" Stein takes a step forward.

"No." Julia cuts her off. For the first time, we look at the girl and see royalty. "This is what we will do. Can you imagine me in safer hands?"

37

LA MAESTRANZA – EASTER SUNDAY, LATE AFTERNOON

Rincón stands at the *barrera*, watching his *peóns* cape the bull. It's a brute. Jet black, two tons of solid muscle, it charges the matadors on legs like steel springs. The sellout crowd, fifteen thousand strong, roars.

The *peón* executes a *verónica*, goes white as the beast passes close enough to brush his *chaleco*.

"My God." Salazar is sweating, not from the heat. "He'll be killed."

"Enough of this," Rincón says. "Get him to the pic."

Salazar signals the *peón*. Relieved, the man capes the bull into position for the picador.

I lean on the *barrera* next to Rincón. "Look at that magnificent animal," the maestro says.

"He's a brute."

"Marinero of Miura," Rincón says. "He was not scheduled to fight today. The bulls prepared last night had to be returned. Today we fight replacements. Some fiercer and more unpredictable than the others. This one is treacherous."

"Why did you have to switch?"

"Vandals broke into the *Maestranza* last night. They entered the *corrales*. Once the bulls have seen a man on foot, they are no good for the *corrida*. That is why the *corrida* was delayed."

It had taken hours to clean up the bullring.

Lance in hand, Allegre advances to the gate. Salazar leans close, grabs the picador's saddle. "Don't spare the beast. Cut the bastard down."

The picador nods, gallops forward on his fine Arabian. Bullfighters want brave bulls. Strong, dangerous, spirited. But not too much. It is the picador's job to weaken the bull enough for the matador to put on a show. But not so much it looks like an unfair fight. It's a fine bit of calibration. Sometimes, if the matador is not at his best, a picador will savage the bull. The crowd hates this, but it makes the matador's job easier.

The *peón* gratefully dodges behind the *barrera*. Leaves the bull to Allegre.

Marinero wheels on the picador and charges. A fighting bull can reach forty miles an hour in a short sprint. He catches Allegre before he's ready. Rams into the horse's body armor with full force. The crowd howls as the horse staggers and the picador is almost thrown from his saddle.

"So this is the animal I must face," Rincón says.

"You don't have to face him," I say.

Rincón turns on me. "What are you saying?"

"Leandro worked for you," I tell him. "*You* killed Ballard and kidnapped Julia."

"Breed, are you crazy?" Rincón tears his eyes away from the spectacle on the *ruedo*. Stares at me with angry eyes.

"Not at all. It took me a while to figure it out. What were those men doing outside the bar in Rodilhan? They were delivering Julia to *you*. Every year, at Semana Santa, you have Leandro kidnap a girl in Arles, hook her on drugs. Spend a week with her in your caravan on the way to Seville. Indulge the sick fantasies you share with Leandro. When you're done, he sells the girl in Morocco."

Marinero rams Allegre a second time, drives the horse and rider against the *barrera*. The picador lances the animal, drives the pic into the hump of muscle right to the *cruceta*. The *cruceta* stops the lance from skewering the bull. Even so, the pic tears a horrible gash in the beast's flesh.

"Breed, you are a fantasist."

"No. The refrigerator in your caravan is packed with morphine. Is it morphine or heroin? Drawers full of syringes."

Instead of pushing against the horse, Marinero withdraws, and the pic slides free. Allegre, who had been leaning against the lance with all his weight, has to fight to keep from toppling from the horse. Quick as lightning, Marinero turns in a half circle and rams the armor a second time. Throws horse and rider against the *barrera* like a heavyweight fighter pinning his opponent against the ropes.

Allegre stabs the bull again. The animal bellows with pain and rage. Backs away, lunges. The picador has had enough, spurs the horse away from the *barrera*.

Rincón turns from me. Watches Allegre gallop back to the gate. "You can prove none of this."

"How did Leandro get my number?"

"What?"

Allegre stops at the gate. "Marinero is a devil," he says. "Even for a Miura. I have never seen an animal like this." Rincón sneers. "He is a mighty bull, but he can be killed like any other."

Salazar wipes sweat from his face. "Cut him down, I tell you. I don't care if he takes three lances."

The second picador advances onto the *ruedo*.

"Leandro called me to demand the ransom," I say. "Only you have my number. He had to get it from you."

"Not I, Breed."

"How did Leandro know Julia was worth thirty million Euros? Only *you* knew Julia was a princess."

Rincón turns on me. "Obviously, someone heard us talking."

"No. I wondered which of your men was a traitor. Because Leandro killed two of them at the castle, they couldn't *all* be involved. I didn't realize till later that *none* of your men were involved. They thought the girls you spent your vacations with were prostitutes. At the castle, Leandro didn't know Julia was a princess. He only wanted to recover his merchandise."

The roar of the crowd is so loud both Rincón and I turn our attention to the ring. Marinero has rammed the second picador. The man lances the bull with such force the *cruceta* snaps. The crowd boos and whistles, but its displeasure is short-lived. Marinero pulls free of the lance and retreats. Paws the sand.

A hush falls over the crowd. The picador should call for a new pic. Without the *cruceta*, the pic he holds can seriously wound or kill the bull. But the man freezes. He has been told to cut Marinero down, and that is what he intends to do.

Rincón starts to sweat. I don't know if he's more affected

by me or Marinero of Miura. I press home my advantage. "I have proof."

"And what might *that* be, Breed?"

"We have Leandro's phones, and we've reviewed all of his calls. *You* called to arrange the kidnapping and ransom. Together, you planned the diversion. A frontal assault to draw us away from the kitchen entrance. Leandro entered the house, came up the stairs. You distracted Ballard in front of Julia's door. Ballard trusted you. I don't know which of you wielded the knife, but it doesn't matter. Either way, you murdered Ballard."

Distracted, Rincon focuses his attention on Marinero. The bull is preparing to attack the picador again.

"Leandro took Julia and made good his escape. He called me to demand the ransom, knew there was a good chance we would geolocate his burner. The Basque's approach was more low-tech. The next morning, he followed us from your ranch, and so did Orlov. You had nothing to do with that."

Rincón appraises me with eyes gone cold.

"Kidnapping and murder," I tell him. "*You* killed Ballard. I wish Spain still used the garrote. I'd love to see you tied to a post and strangled."

Marinero charges the picador. Strikes the horse with terrific acceleration, slams him into the *barrera*. The pic sinks deep. The bull ducks his head, slips the lance, and drives his horns under the body armor. With a powerful thrust of his neck, Marinero gores the animal and lifts horse and rider high onto the fence. The top planks splinter and explode from the *barrera*.

The horse is impaled on the horns. The bull jerks his head left and right, opening the animal's bowels. The rider tries to drive the lance in a third time, but can't get the angle.

Like a weightlifter, Marinero thrusts with his powerful legs, tosses his head, and throws both horse and rider over the *barrera*. Spectators overlooking the passageway recoil with horror.

The crowd is on its feet.

"What a magnificent beast." Rincón whirls away from me, faces his team. Behind them, in the opening of the tunnel, Stein waits with two Spanish police officers and a plain clothes inspector.

Heth sits in the front row of the bleachers, overlooking the *barrera*. I didn't tell her my suspicions, but I had to tell Stein. I needed her to square it with the Spanish police.

Rincón snorts, steps to one of his *banderilleros*. From the man's hands, he snatches a pair of the two-foot barbed stakes.

"Are you insane?" Salazar grabs Rincón by the arm. "Even with two more lances, that animal will kill anything that moves. He's strong, and he's *learning*."

Rincón jerks his arm free. "I have waited my entire *life* for a beast like this."

The matador pushes past his manager and steps into the ring. "*¡Hoy! ¡Toro!*"

The crowd roars. Marinero needs no red *muleta* to induce him to attack. That in itself bodes ill for the matador. The bull charges from thirty yards. Bulls are supposed to be near-sighted, but this one sees just fine.

Rincón stands perfectly still as the bull bears down on him. He holds the *banderillas* over his head, one in each hand. They are adorned with bright yellow and orange ribbons. When it seems too late to escape, Rincón steps aside and places the stakes perfectly in the animal's hump. The crowd screams with one voice. "*¡Olé!*"

Marinero charges on. He missed Rincón by inches. *Peóns* dart into the ring, distract the animal with their capes before ducking for cover behind the *barrera*. Rincón stands straight, shoulders thrown back. He extends his hand imperiously. Salazar hands him two more *banderillas*.

Fists to her mouth, Heth rises to her feet.

The barbs are meant to enrage a bull weakened by the pics. Marinero does not appear to have been weakened at all. Rincón steps before him, *banderillas* raised. "*¡Hoy! ¡Toro!*"

The bull charges a second time. Again, Rincón waits till the last instant to spring aside. He catapults himself into the air and shoots the darts into the hump of muscle. The shoulder of the great beast brushes the man and knocks him to one side. Not the best placement, but by now, the crowd will forgive Rincón anything.

Once again, the *peóns* distract the bull. Rincón dusts himself off. Blood from the bull's wounds has smeared the side of his *chaleco*. Intoxicated by the adulation of the crowd, he strides back to the *puerta de cuadrillas*. Stares at me with contempt, takes the *estoque* and *muleta* from Salazar. The killing sword and cape. Normally, the *faena*, or artistic performance, is executed with a fake sword, because the *estoque* is heavy. I don't know if Rincón is going to kill the bull right away.

The matador strides to the center of the *ruedo*. There, far away from the *barrera*, there is no place to hide. He drapes the *muleta* over the *estoque*.

"*¡Hoy! ¡Toro!*" Rincón shakes the *muleta*.

Marinero trots toward Rincón, accelerates to a canter, then charges at a full gallop. The matador stands his ground, waits for the animal. When the beast reaches him, Rincón raises the *muleta* ever so slightly. The animal's horns slice past, missing him by inches.

"*¡Olé!*" the crowd yells.

Rincón draws Marinero into pass after pass. Rather than tiring, the bull becomes more enraged.

"Devil," Salazar says. "The beast is *possessed*." The manager screams at Rincón. "Kill it, Maestro! Kill it now!"

Rincón stares at Salazar. There is no good time to kill this bull. It has not been weakened by the pics. Can he kill it? Normally, the thrust of death is delivered when the bull is exhausted. The *corrida* was never meant to be a fair fight. The odds are always on the side of the man. Today, they are on the side of the bull.

Enraged, adrenaline surging through his blood, Marinero is strong enough to charge. Indeed, the beast is learning the man's tricks. Kill it now, and the fight will assure Rincón immortality. A place in history with men like Manolete and Arruza.

The bull paws the sand. Its black flanks are shiny with blood. The *banderillas*, orange and yellow, bob on the cruel barbs planted in its flesh. Rincón raises the *muleta* to draw its attention. Sights down the blade. A useless exercise at fifteen yards. It's all show for the bloodthirsty crowd. Rincón means to have the blade ready when the beast is upon him, when he can adjust his aim at the last moment.

"*No, no.*" The crowd realizes what he is doing. Mutters with disbelief. The spectators shout "*No*," but they *want* the spectacle. They *demand* drama. They fall silent when they realize history is about to be made. They have the good fortune to bear witness.

Marinero charges. Rincón has the skill and agility to

place the *banderillas*. Surely he has the skill to place the *estoque*.

The bull is like a boxer. Rincón has watched him lead with his right horn, then attack with the left. Rincón is aware of Marinero's treacherous nature, but has no choice. He has to play to the animal's established pattern. When the bull is within striking distance, the matador rises on his toes.

Marinero leads with his left. Rincón lunges over the beast's head, drives the *estoque* between its shoulders and into the heart. But the matador springs to the left—the wrong direction. The devil, Marinero, attacks with his right horn. Rincón leaps directly into the thrust.

The point slices into Rincón's belly. Marinero, dying, jerks his great head. Thrusts the long horn through the matador's diaphragm, left lung, and heart. Lifts him off his feet. The pair freeze—the bull, skewered by the *estoque*, the man impaled on the horn. Then the beast's powerful legs give way and it collapses onto the sand, dragging the dead man on top of him.

A collective gasp from the crowd, and silence falls on the *Maestranza*. Normally, there is a rush to aid a fallen matador, to carry him to the infirmary. There is no question here. No man could survive such a wound inflicted by that great horn.

Salazar steps around the *barrera* and runs toward the man and bull. Both figures slump, motionless. They seem forever locked in an embrace of death.

I push off from the *barrera* and join Stein. She's staring at the tableau with distaste. In the bleachers, Heth's shoulders slump. She wanted to see a bullfight. This *corrida* will go down in history, but to tell the story, a man had to die.

A Spanish story, a tragedy. There are *no* happy fucking endings.

Black Sun

"He cheated us," Stein says.

"How do you figure that?"

"His victims deserved justice."

Stein's right. No one will hear about Rincón's crimes.

"We could write tomorrow's headlines." I walk along the tunnel, and Stein falls in next to me. "Javier Rincón will take his place among the immortals."

"So will Marinero," Stein says. "They'll mount his head on the museum wall."

"Next to Islero of Miura, he who slew the great Manolete."

We walk together through the *puerta principe*.

Heth joins us in front of the Maestranza. She's out of breath. Had to fight her way through the crowd to reach us. She rushes to me, eyes pleading. "Is he dead?"

"Yes. If there was any chance, they would rush him to the infirmary."

The girl shakes her head. "*That's not supposed to happen.*"

"Bullfights aren't as one-sided as people think. The maestro was gored fourteen times, and any number of those wounds could have killed him. Today, Marinero was tougher than the maestro and his team."

Stein and I agreed to say nothing about Rincón's guilt. Now that he is gone, the Spanish police will let the matter die with him.

"Rincón wanted this," I tell Heth. "He wanted to become immortal."

There are two black limos waiting in a VIP lane cordoned off by Spanish police. Orlov, Takigawa and Julia wait in one of them. I walk with Stein and Heth toward the vehicles.

"Princess Julia spoke with Tibor Szabo for two hours,"

Stein says. "He's held conversations with the State Department and the Foreign Ministry of the Russian Federation."

"Is a resolution in sight?"

"The coup has failed. The regent and Princess Julia are alive. The United States and the Russian Federation will jointly guarantee Marethia's neutrality."

I let out a breath. "Sounds like everybody gets what they want."

"Like most things," Stein says, "it's a compromise. I think you'll always be welcome in Marethia."

One of the limos will take Orlov, Julia and myself to the airport. We have first-class tickets to Budapest. From Morón, Stein and Takigawa will fly home. Together, they will escort Ballard's casket. Heth will wait for me in Seville. When Julia is safe with the regent, I will return to finish my vacation.

Behind us, the *Maestranza* shakes with the roar of fifteen thousand voices. Rincón's body is being carried from the *ruedo*.

What Rincón told me is true.

At the *corrida*, the most dangerous beast is the crowd.

The End

ACKNOWLEDGMENTS

BLACK SUN would not have been possible without the support, encouragement, and guidance of my agent, Ivan Mulcahy, of MMB Creative. I would also like to thank my publishers, Brian Lynch and Garret Ryan of Inkubator Books for seeing the novel's potential. Garret, in particular, provided a great sounding board and his editorial efforts are much appreciated.

Thanks go to Claire Milto of Inkubator Books for her support in the novel's launch. The novel also benefitted from the invaluable feedback of members of my writing group and Beta readers.

If you could spend a moment to write an honest review, no matter how short, I would be extremely grateful. They really do help readers discover my books.

Feel free to contact me at cameron.curtis545@gmail.com. I'd love to hear from you.

ALSO BY CAMERON CURTIS

Made in the USA
Monee, IL
14 October 2023

44598564R00152